THE SHOW MUST GO ON

Slocum found himself caught up in Lily's flow of honeyed phrases, carried along to wherever she wanted to take him. Then all hell broke loose.

A first, then a second bullet ripped through the air and tore the scenery behind Lily. This got Slocum moving, fighting his way through the stampede of miners, all intent on getting the hell out of the saloon.

"Down!" Slocum shouted at Lily. "Get down!" His words were swallowed up in the thunder of feet. He fought his way through the crowd, going against the stream of men. The smell of spilled beer mixed with the coppery tang of freshly spilled blood. He saw Lily on the stage, her bright blue eyes wide. She jerked to one side and yelped as a bullet sang a song more deadly than any the chanteuse had ever warbled.

Slocum kept getting slammed against the bar. He grunted and heaved, jumping onto the long oak bar. He stumbled, got to his feet, then slipped in the spilled beer again. Hanging precariously from broken hinges were masked men firing their six-shooters. Slocum's quick eyes went from the gunmen to their target. He had thought a liquored-up cowboy might have started it all, but these two were anything but drunk. They were trying to kill Lily . . .

JAKE LOGAN

SLOCUM AND LADY DEATH

J

JOVE BOOKS, NEW YORK

THE BERKLEY PUBLISHING GROUP
Published by the Penguin Group
Penguin Group (USA) Inc.
375 Hudson Street, New York, New York 10014, USA
Penguin Group (Canada), 90 Eglinton Avenue East, Suite 700, Toronto, Ontario M4P 2Y3, Canada
(a division of Pearson Penguin Canada Inc.)
Penguin Books Ltd., 80 Strand, London WC2R 0RL, England
Penguin Group Ireland, 25 St. Stephen's Green, Dublin 2, Ireland (a division of Penguin Books Ltd.)
Penguin Group (Australia), 250 Camberwell Road, Camberwell, Victoria 3124, Australia
(a division of Pearson Australia Group Pty. Ltd.)
Penguin Books India Pvt. Ltd., 11 Community Centre, Panchsheel Park, New Delhi—110 017, India
Penguin Group (NZ), Cnr. Airborne and Rosedale Roads, Albany, Auckland 1310, New Zealand
(a division of Pearson New Zealand Ltd.)
Penguin Books (South Africa) (Pty.) Ltd., 24 Sturdee Avenue, Rosebank, Johannesburg 2196,
South Africa

Penguin Books Ltd., Registered Offices: 80 Strand, London WC2R 0RL, England

This is a work of fiction. Names, characters, places, and incidents either are the product of the author's imagination or are used fictitiously, and any resemblance to actual persons, living or dead, business establishments, events, or locales is entirely coincidental.

SLOCUM AND LADY DEATH

A Jove Book / published by arrangement with the author

PRINTING HISTORY
Jove edition / September 2005

ISBN: 0-515-14010-4

JOVE®
Jove Books are published by The Berkley Publishing Group,
a division of Penguin Group (USA) Inc.,
375 Hudson Street, New York, New York 10014.
JOVE is a registered trademark of Penguin Group (USA) Inc.
The "J" design is a trademark belonging to Penguin Group (USA) Inc.

PRINTED IN THE UNITED STATES OF AMERICA

10 9 8 7 6 5 4 3 2 1

1

John Slocum hardly noticed the bitter taste of the warm beer in front of him or that the vile brew had cost two bits. He was too intent on the show sweeping back and forth with manic energy on stage at Tombstone's largest and gaudiest saloon, the Gala Whiskey Emporium. The smoky footlights cast peculiar shadows against the backdrop and the side curtains, but again Slocum wasn't looking at any of that. His sharp green eyes focused solely on the busty blonde in the center of the stage belting out one song after another, surrounded by dancers who weren't shy about showing their legs and hindquarters as they trotted about.

Lily Montrechet wasn't much of a singer. She couldn't act her way through the simplest of scenes. But those weren't the attributes that kept Slocum watching. She was a star and no matter how good her performance or how bad, she *made* everyone in the audience watch her simply by walking from the wings. Even better, Slocum had met Lily a month earlier in Denver and had helped her out of a pickle. They had traveled together since then, and Lily had shown her appreciation constantly for all Slocum had done.

"She's some looker, ain't she?" muttered the drunk miner crowded close to Slocum at the bar. "Wouldn't mind doin' some hard-rock minin' in her stope."

Slocum glanced at the man and saw he meant nothing by it. He was as appreciative of Lily's . . . skills . . . as any of the other women-starved men crowded shoulder-to-shoulder into the Gala's large theater. If anything, Slocum not only took no offense, but also felt a touch of pride. Lily was his woman, as much as any woman could be.

He heaved a deep sigh as he watched her move slowly from one side of the stage to the other and back as the dancers exited to leave her alone. The blonde turned this way and that to best show off her charms, magnified into massive shadows on the backdrop by the footlights. Of all the women he had known in his years drifting through the West, she was special. Maybe not special enough to think on settling down. Or maybe so.

Slocum knew there was little chance Lily would demand any such commitment from him at the moment since she was pursuing her own career on the stage, and doing well. She had been the headliner at the Gala for a week, and the men had yet to tire of her or her somewhat shrill singing. Again, Slocum understood. Her quick smile and the twinkle in her azure-blue eyes, the set to her body, and the way she could look at a man so intimately that he was certain he was the only one in the universe made her special.

Lily's song came to a grating end, and she began reciting from some play or other. Or, as Slocum believed, she simply made up what she said to match the mood of the crowd. Some nights it was done in a husky whisper, like he was used to hearing when she lay beside him during the long nights. Other nights she shrieked and ranted and raved, storming about the stage as if she had gone quite mad. Tonight she spoke clearly, her words carrying like a thistle on the wind to each and every man in the saloon for his personal appreciation.

Slocum found himself caught up in the swift flow of honeyed phrases, carried along to wherever Lily wanted to take him. Then all hell broke loose.

For a moment Slocum was not certain what was going on. He was almost hypnotized by the woman's stirring delivery of a soliloquy from some play she claimed was popular on the Continent. Then a second bullet ripped through the air and tore a chunk out of the scenery behind Lily. This got Slocum moving, fighting his way through the stampede of miners all intent on getting the hell out of the saloon and to safety, wherever that might be since few of them carried six-shooters and even fewer saw who was doing the shooting.

"Down!" Slocum shouted at Lily. "Get down!" His words were swallowed up in the thunder of feet crashing down hard on the plank floorboards and the loud shouts of frightened men. Everything crashed together in Slocum's mind as he fought his way through the crowd, going against the stream of men forcing their way to safety as more shots rang out. The smell of spilled beer mixed with the coppery tang of freshly spilled blood. Cries of fear turned to moans of pain. Worst of all, Slocum felt as if he swam upstream against the raging Colorado River, weakening by the moment but knowing he could never stop trying.

He saw Lily on the stage, looking perplexed. Then her bright blue eyes widened; she jerked to one side and yelped as a bullet sang a song more deadly than any the chanteuse had ever warbled. Seeing her in peril like this, Slocum stopped trying to reach her, and let the tide of miners and cowboys rush past him so he could work his way toward a rough-hewn plank wall. The idea was easier to think up than the deed was easy to accomplish.

Too many miners were too panicked. Slocum kept getting slammed against the bar until he realized this was a message. He grunted and heaved, forcing a short, stocky miner who smelled like Giant Blasting Powder and beer away far enough so Slocum could jump onto the long oak plank that served as a bar. He knocked over shot glasses and beer mugs, but hardly noticed as he sent hunks of broken glass flying in his wake. He stumbled, got to his feet, slipped in the spilled beer again, then came to his knees as he surveyed the still-crowded saloon.

Across the room on either side of the main doors, now

hanging precariously from broken hinges, stood masked men with their six-shooters out and firing wildly. Slocum's quick eyes went from the gunmen to their target.

He went cold inside. He had thought that a cowboy might have gotten liquored up and decided to hurrah the Gala Whiskey Emporium. These two were anything but drunk, in spite of the abandon with which they fired. They were trying to kill Lily.

Slocum leveled his own six-gun and fired. His first shot took off the tall-crowned hat of a peddler come to town to sell his wares and get a few drinks under his belt. Slocum had spoken to the man a few seconds before Lily's show had begun. Slocum was sorry for the hole he put in the hat, but paid it no never mind as he shot a second time. This round dug out a huge hole in the wall behind the gunman closest to Slocum. For a second, the masked man seemed confused, then saw his danger.

He swung his six-shooter around, but Slocum gave him no chance to get the range. The third time Slocum fired, he hit his target. The gunman yelped loud enough to be heard above the din. He cursed a blue streak as he clutched his right hand. Slocum didn't bother with a killing shot. He had forced the man to drop his pistol. Slocum swung to get a bead on the second man shooting at Lily, but had no chance. The man grabbed one of the whores and used the screaming woman as a shield.

Then Slocum had his hands full of men shooting at him, mistaken in their belief he was responsible for all the furor. Two gamblers used some of their hardware to make it very hot and very dangerous to remain standing exposed to their gunfire. Slocum dived behind the bar and moved in a crouch to the end, slipped under, and pressed hard against the wall to the right of the stage.

"Lily!" he shouted again at the woman, who cowered behind a stagehand who had taken a bullet to the belly and lay curled into a fetal position, groaning in pain. The blonde poked her head up, eyes wide with fear.

"John!"

"Stay down!" The masked man near the door opened fire again, his aim improving as he got the range.

Slocum kicked over a chair and jumped on it, trying for a good shot. The saloon had finally cleared out, but the gunman still clung to the Cyprian, preventing Slocum from getting a clear shot. He wasn't above cutting down the woman to get to the killer. In the long run this would save more lives, but Slocum knew he was running out of ammo in his six-shooter.

Jumping from the chair, Slocum cleared the edge of the stage and hit hard, rolling over and coming up beside Lily Montrechet. He grabbed her arm and roughly pulled her around behind him, using himself as a screen.

"To the right," he said. Slocum was happy to see that Lily followed orders without asking foolish questions. He scuttled ahead of her, keeping as close to the stage as he could to minimize himself as a target. The remaining gunman had reloaded, shoved aside the screaming whore, and was walking forward, firing more accurately than ever.

Slocum sucked in his breath, lowered his head, and ran as hard as he could off the stage and into the saloon wall. For a ghastly moment Slocum thought the wall would hold. Then he felt the thin planks yield and the nails came free with a soul-searing screech. He tumbled into the alley beside the Gala, Lily almost on top of him as she followed.

"Get to the stables," Slocum said, coming to his feet and waiting for the gunman to poke his head through the hole in the saloon wall. He relaxed a mite when the head never popped through. That gave them the chance to get out of Tombstone and leave this ruckus behind them. Slocum backed away, checked to be sure that no one popped around the corner of the Gala Whiskey Emporium, and then dashed after Lily. It wasn't in his blood to run from a fight, but this didn't have anything to do with him.

Seeing Lily ahead of him made Slocum wonder if it had anything to do with her. The problem in Denver had been a dispute between her and a theater owner who insisted her contract be renewed at the same rate after she had asked for more money. When they had been unable to reach an agreement, Lily Montrechet had tried to move on to a competing theater. The first theater owner had gotten nasty and shot the manager of the second theater. That was when Slocum had gotten mixed up in the fray.

At least that was the story Lily had given him, and he had believed her. The manager of the second theater was undeniably dead, and this had given more credence to her version of what had happened. Slocum looked over his shoulder to be certain the gunmen from the Gala weren't on their heels. Something told him these two were after Lily. The way they had opened fire at the stage told him she was the target, even if the stagehand had caught a round in the belly.

"Where are we going, John?"

Slocum looked up at Lily. Her face was smeared with dirt, her blond hair was in wild disarray, and her clothing was torn in places. She had never looked lovelier or more appealing.

"You want to hang around Tombstone?" he asked.

"The critics are a bit too harsh here, my dear," Lily said, her chin lifting upward as she struck a pose. "My performance wasn't that bad."

"Somewhere else, then," Slocum said, climbing into the saddle. He turned his mare's head and headed out of town, away from the Gala and the flock of lawmen heading for it.

"It must be somewhere special," Lily said haughtily. "Somewhere they can admire me and appreciate my talents."

"You've got *me* for that," Slocum said, eliciting a laugh from Lily's bow-shaped lips.

"That's why I love you, John. You don't put up with my bullshit." Laughing even more heartily, she put her heels to the sides of her horse and trotted from town.

"Bisbee," Slocum said as they got beyond the last ramshackle buildings around Tombstone and he spotted a battered signpost. "That's where we're heading."

"A fine place, so I've been told," Lily said, her good humor restored entirely. "One where they won't take potshots at a performer who displeases them. I have a friend there who might see fit to help, or so I hope."

Slocum said nothing for a few minutes, thinking back on what he had seen during the shoot-out. He finally had to ask, "Did you know them?"

"Who?" Lily didn't turn to look at him when she spoke. Slocum tensed at this evasion. He had played enough poker—and heard enough lies—to anticipate when someone was going to try to slide half-truths past him with sweet talk. "Oh, you mean those awful men back at the saloon. I can't say, really."

Lily had used all the inflections she employed while on stage. She knew them, and Slocum wasn't going to let the matter lie. Their lives might depend on getting to the truth. The entire truth.

"Who were they? You know them."

"Oh, John, you can be so persistent." Lily saw he wasn't going to let her put him off. She heaved a deep sigh, causing her ample bosoms to jiggle delightfully. Slocum knew she did this on purpose to distract him. As agreeable as it was watching her, even simply riding along, he wanted to get to the heart of the matter. He could sightsee later.

"Did you know them in Denver?"

"Yes," she said. "I did. They were employees of that terrible Mr. Slattery."

"No, they weren't," Slocum said. "I don't care how mad a theater owner might be over his star performer leaving. He isn't sending a pair of killers all the way to Arizona to put a couple slugs into you. It's not worth it. Who were they?"

"I didn't get a good look at either of them . . ."

"Lily, we part company right now if you don't tell me. I won't listen to you lying, no matter how you sugarcoat it. Straight out, no frills. The truth."

"You can be so hard at times, John. I like that in a man." She batted her long eyelashes in his direction, and saw her little wordplay did nothing to melt his resolve. "Oh, very well. I don't know their names, not exactly. One is called

Clay, but I never heard his last name. The other is Utah
Jack Vernon. I heard that name during a poker game I happened to observe."

"Utah Jack Vernon?" Slocum's lips thinned to a razor-
slash. "He's killed a half-dozen men."

"Oh, I doubt that. He is such a braggart. Seldom have I
seen anyone not in the theater who can spin such yarns
about himself. I doubt Jack's killed more than two or three
men, and he's probably shot them all in the back. That's
more his style."

"He brags on the men he killed?" This bothered
Slocum. Not that Utah Jack Vernon was a killer, but that he
probably enjoyed it. Slocum killed when he had to, but he
wasn't inclined to gun a man down without looking him in
the eye. And he never talked about the men he had killed,
from the very first one he had shot in battle during the war
to the last who had crossed him.

"He is a very colorful talker, making me believe he's
making up most of what he says," Lily replied.

"How'd you run afoul of him and this Clay fellow?"

"Oh, a mutual acquaintance, that's all. We were out in
San Francisco; then I left that fine town and went to Denver. That's about the time we met, John. You are so much
more handsome than him."

"Who's him?"

"Now, John, do you think I am the kind to kiss and tell?
Besides, we parted on good terms. Very good terms," she
said, grinning broadly. "If you know what I mean."

"There weren't any hard feelings on the part of this fellow in San Francisco?"

"Not after I left."

Slocum knew when he heard the truth—and when he
got only a portion of it. There was a powerful lot more to
Lily's story than she was telling, but he wasn't inclined to
press the matter too far. But there were a couple points he
had to clear up fast.

"Why are they after you? Utah Jack and Clay?"

"I told you, John. I don't know. I never had much to do

with either of them. They were hired hands, not important folks at all. They certainly were not friends of his, that's for certain. Just employees and not good ones."

"Employees who kill for a living?"

"Why must you be so blunt?" Lily sniffed to show her disdain for such questions, then said, "I suppose you could say that. They never killed anyone while I was with him."

"That's the other question I want an answer for. Who's this gentleman friend of yours? The one in San Francisco?"

"I called him Big Willie. And that's all I will say. It is an affront, an invasion of a lady's privacy, to ask more. Unless you no longer look upon me as a lady. If that is so, John, we *shall* part company here and now."

"You really don't know why two gunmen would want to kill you? Or this Big Willie? He definitely doesn't want you filled with lead and left for the buzzards?"

"How colorful," she said. Then the blonde shook her head. "Cross my heart and hope to die, John. The last I saw of them all was in San Francisco. I have no idea why Clay and Jack were in Tombstone or why they might want to do me harm."

Slocum heard the ring of sincerity and decided Lily wasn't a good enough actress to make him believe an outright lie. She might embroider and sugarcoat and try to worm around the truth, but this was an outright statement that sounded like the truth.

"It'll be a couple days before we reach Bisbee," he told her. She looked at him sharply, her bright blue eyes fixed hard on him. She smiled almost shyly.

"Thank you, John. I won't disappoint you."

"That's the farthest thing from my mind," he said.

"Your mind's not what I was talking about." Lily laughed, and put her heels to her horse's flanks and galloped ahead. Slocum knew they would kill their horses if they galloped along for very long in the darkness, but that wasn't what Lily intended. She wanted him to catch her, and he did.

Afterward, Slocum lay with his arm around the

woman's bare shoulders, more asleep than awake. She had been true to her word about not disappointing after they had found this small oasis in the middle of the Arizona desert. They had pitched camp, tended the horses, eaten a light meal, and drunk their fill from the watering hole, then set about to exploring one another's bodies until they had drifted off to sleep hours earlier.

Slocum reckoned it was almost dawn and time to get moving along the road to Bisbee. He had snaked his arm free of Lily's shoulders and rolled to one side when he heard the metallic sound of a hammer cocking. He grabbed for his still-holstered Colt beside him on the ground when the shot rang out. Lily made a soft sighing sound. Then there was no sound at all.

He pulled upright and swung his six-gun around, hunting for their assailant. Only distant noises of animals stirring uneasily from their burrows to hunt and be hunted reached his ears. No second shot, no telltale movement in the brush around them. Slocum relaxed and shoved his gun back into the holster.

"You won't believe this," he said. "I just had a bad dream and thought somebody was shooting at us."

Slocum turned and looked at the woman beside him. The blanket had been pulled away from her torso when he reached for his six-shooter. A small round hole in her left breast leaked a few drops of blood, and the rhythmic rise and fall of her bountiful chest was stilled. Life had been stolen away by that single shot that had not been a dream but a nightmare.

2

Dawn poked pink and gray fingers above the mountains to the east, but Slocum was not interested in such beauty. He wanted to find the trail of the man who had brutally murdered Lily in her sleep. Careful to keep low and not present a good target himself, Slocum dressed, and then became bolder as he explored the area around the watering hole. After ten minutes he came to the conclusion that the murderer was long gone. The bushwhacker had fired the single round into Lily's white, beating breast and then had slunk off, back to whatever hole he had crawled out of.

What bothered Slocum most was how the single shot had robbed Lily of her life, but there had not been a second to kill him. Slocum had been vulnerable and would never have been able to locate their assailant and return fire before the rest of the rifle's rounds found their way to his head and heart. That meant the killer had wanted only Lily dead. He might have fired, seen he had missed Slocum, and panicked, but Slocum didn't think so. The man's silent, expert departure told as much of his abilities as the accuracy of the shot.

The ambusher had intended to kill Lily—and had with cold-blooded ease.

Why? Slocum remembered the attack in the saloon, and tried to figure out how it fit in. The two masked men had been firing at the stage. He had thought they were just drunks at first, but then realized they intended to kill Lily then and there. Failing, had they trailed her out of Tombstone all the way to this watering hole?

A hard determination settled about Slocum. Nobody slaughtered a beautiful woman like that and got away with it.

It took the better part of a half hour for him to locate the spot where the killer had stood. Slocum judged distances and how hard it would have been to fire a rifle in the dark to kill Lily with the single shot. He was up against a crack marksman. No amount of luck would have allowed a shot like that. Skill. Lots of gun-handling skill had been responsible for the beautiful woman's death.

Slocum saddled and followed the trail to the sunbaked, hard dirt road. Here he could not tell if the killer had gone back to Tombstone or if he had ridden on to Bisbee. Worse, Slocum found it impossible to tell if there had been others riding with the assassin. The best hoofprints in the thin dust hinted that a solitary rider had gone toward Bisbee. Having nothing better to go on, Slocum trotted in that direction, turning over and over in his mind all the possibilities. As much as he hated to admit it, he had to tell the law about Lily's murder because he was unable to go any farther himself. The only possible clue he had was the one owlhoot he had winged back at the Gala Whiskey Emporium—and how many men in a wild, open mining territory like Arizona had bandaged arms?

It took less time than he anticipated reaching Bisbee. The town was a miniature of Tombstone, but without any of the charm. Fewer adobe buildings, fewer people, less money flowing because of mining. It was a border town far enough removed from the border to make it nothing more than squalid, in spite of the burgeoning copper- and gold-mining operations east of town in the Mule Mountains.

Slocum had no trouble finding the sheriff's office smack in the center of town next to the bank. He dismounted, brushed trail dust off his hat and face, then went inside. The day was getting hot outside, but in the thick-walled mud brick jailhouse it was cool and dim and quiet.

The sheriff looked up from a week-old copy of the *Tombstone Epitaph* he was reading. From the way he scowled at Slocum, he wasn't too inclined to take kindly to being disturbed for no good reason. Seeing this, Slocum got to the point.

"A woman's been murdered outside town," he said. "Her name's Lily Montrechet and—"

"Outside town, you say?"

"Yeah. She—"

"You do it?" The sheriff cast a gimlet eye on Slocum, as if expecting him to confess then and there.

"That's about the dumbest question I ever heard," Slocum said angrily. "If I'd murdered her, why'd I come to tell you to find her killer?"

"Some might think it was a clever thing to do. Throw suspicion off themselves. Others, like you maybe, you might think it was a cheeky, audacious thing to do. Poke some fun at ole Sheriff Yarrow."

"Or I might just be a citizen come to report a murder."

"You might," the sheriff said, turning back to his paper.

"Are you going to ride out to see what happened?"

"Now why the hell am I s'pposed to do that, mister? You say she's dead. I can't bring her back to life. If you rode very far, there's nothin' I can do to find the varmint what killed her. 'Less you're changin' your tune and decide to confess."

"You're not even going to ride out to examine the body?"

"You said she's dead. How'm I gonna change that?"

"She was murdered."

"Not in Bisbee. The town's not got a marshal right now. Bit of a hard time with the city treasury after the mayor rode off with it a while back. No one's damn fool dumb enough to take a job like that when there's no money for salary. So you see, as sheriff of Cochise County, I got to stick close to keep the peace within the city limits. This

14   JAKE LOGAN

here's where most folks are and where the law needs enforcin' the most."

Slocum held his anger in check. He stepped back from the littered desk and squared his shoulders. This caught the lawman's attention. Sheriff Yarrow's eyes widened and his mouth opened a tad, as if he wanted to say something but fear choked it off. He obviously thought Slocum was going to throw down on him.

"You won't do anything about Miss Montrechet's death, then I will. Is that all right with you, Sheriff?"

"I . . . do what you want, only you get out of Bisbee and don't bother comin' back."

"I'll let you know what happens," Slocum said, ignoring the lawman's threat. He backed off another pace, then opened the door and left, emerging into the hot noonday sun. He had been wrong coming to Bisbee to fetch the law. He saw that now. Slocum swung into the saddle and rode down the main street until he came to the general store. He bent over, grabbed a short-handled shovel, and hefted it.

The proprietor came out, squinted at Slocum, and said, "That'll be two dollars, mister."

"Send the bill to Sheriff Yarrow," Slocum said. "I'm doing some work for him."

"But the city ain't got no money. You—"

Slocum rode off, leaving the store clerk to sputter, bluster, and futilely shake his fist in the air. So far, Slocum wasn't favorably impressed with Bisbee, and doubted staying longer would change his opinion one iota. He rode fast back along the road, and reached the watering hole with a couple hours of daylight left. Letting his horse drink, careful that it wouldn't take in so much water from the pool that it began to bloat, Slocum went to where he had left Lily.

He had wrapped her body in a blanket and then had piled rocks over her, not wanting to bury her because he had mistakenly thought the sheriff would come out and want to examine the body for whatever he could find that would identify her killer. Slocum saw coyote tracks all around, but the scavengers had not had time to work away the rocks to get to the corpse.

Slocum hunted for an appropriate spot, and found it atop a hill some distance away. He began digging in the hard, rocky ground until his back ached. With every scoop of soil he tossed onto the pile beside the deepening hole, he got madder and madder. It was his lot in life to ride with death. Lily being cut down the way she had been was wrong. Slocum accepted the risks, but the woman had been an innocent bystander.

Slocum straightened, dropped his shovel, and then laughed out loud. There had been nothing innocent about Lily Montrechet. She had been lusty, even bawdy, and about the finest companion Slocum had found to bed. But innocent? Slocum doubted Lily had even been born that way. Then he quieted down a mite. However she had lived her life, she did not deserve to die this way.

Wiping sweat from his forehead, he returned to the watering hole and hefted the blanket-wrapped body over his shoulder. Lugging it up the hill took what remained of his energy. Slocum lowered the body into the grave, then began returning the dirt and rock to the hole. When he had finished, he piled what stones he could find atop the soft earth to keep the coyotes from digging her up. Six feet under. That was the minimum depth where animals could no longer smell a body and come for it, claws scrabbling to dig up a meal. Slocum hadn't been able to bury Lily that deep, but this would do. In a week or two the sun would bake the ground into a hardness unmatched by anything this side of a kiln-fired pot.

Slocum settled down on his haunches and stared at the grave, wondering if he ought to fashion a marker. He looked up, saw the evening star and the setting sun just under it, and knew they would serve better than a cross or something else that Lily would never have permitted had she been alive. Still, he said a few words of prayer he remembered hearing so many times during the war, then trudged down the hill to the watering hole.

Slocum stripped to the waist and washed off trail dust and, to his surprise, blood. Lily's blood. He had smeared just a bit of the few drops from her breast onto his when he bent over to look at her. This caused him to scrub more furiously, as if he might be somehow infected by the red spots. Slocum finished and sank back, supported against his saddle, staring at the stars stretched across the Arizona night sky. Wisps of thin clouds blocked out some of the stars, like scars across the heavens, but Slocum wasn't looking at the ghost-lighted clouds or the diamond stars. He was seeing himself with a six-shooter in his hand, delivering justice to the murderer who had shot Lily in her sleep.

Tracking down the man responsible was going to be a chore, but Slocum vowed to do it. He owed it to Lily and he owed it to himself to find out why another man would shoot a helpless woman.

As he thought on the matter, he began drifting off to sleep, exhausted from his day of riding and digging. Somewhere near midnight, though, he came awake with a start. Slocum had gone through the war by listening to this sixth sense when it warned him of someone nearby. Now it wasn't whispering in his ear. It was screaming. Without moving about too much, he drew his Colt and laid it across his lap. He was still half-flopped over his saddle and his horse dozed a few yards away, hobbles in place on the front legs.

Seeing the horse so peaceful and undisturbed made Slocum think he was having another nightmare, but he remembered the last one he thought he'd had. It had turned out to be stark reality. He peered into the darkness, wondering if an animal stirred.

One did. And it was human.

Slocum saw the indistinct form raise up from behind a clump of prickly pear cactus and take on more recognizable features. To his surprise, a second man joined the first, and they huddled together and exchanged whispers that were undoubtedly about Slocum. He put his thumb on the hammer of his six-gun and slid his forefinger onto the trigger. Then Slocum did about the hardest thing ever. He waited.

The two men parted silently, one circling to the east and the other coming from the west to catch him in a cross fire. Slocum waited for one to get closer than the other, then sat bolt upright, swung his six-gun around, and fired in a smooth motion. A foot-long flash arrowed from the muzzle, slower to follow the bullet going down the barrel, but preceding the groan of pain as Slocum hit his target.

Not waiting to see what the other man would do, Slocum dug his heels into the ground and somersaulted backward over his saddle to land hard on his belly. He got his six-shooter into position and fired where he thought the second man might be. No rewarding cry of pain came, telling him he had misjudged. He waited for the wounded man to call to his partner.

When the expected plea for help came, Slocum fired again. No response, but he had the gut feeling there wouldn't be one. He had killed the sneaking back-shooter.

"He got me," Slocum whispered, trying to make his voice low enough to be heard but not loud enough to be identified. He hoped to lure the second gunman out of hiding with this ploy. The trick didn't work. The man was either too scared or too wily to fall for it.

Wiggling on his belly, Slocum got to the edge of the watering hole and tried to find where the second man might be hiding. The hoofbeats pounding away from the watering hole told Slocum the man had hightailed it fast when his partner had been cut down.

He got to his feet and went exploring to find the first desperado. He almost tripped over the outlaw's dead body in the dark. Dropping to one knee, Slocum rolled the man over and stared at the slack features. If he had ever seen the man before, he couldn't remember when. A quick search of the man's pockets didn't turn up much. A few greenbacks stuffed into his shirt pocket went into Slocum's. A punched train ticket from El Paso to Bisbee showed where the man had come from. In the starlight Slocum was hard-pressed to read the date on the ticket stub. He thrust this into his pocket to look at later in daylight. It might not mean anything, but it could tell him something about the identity of the second man. Asking around the railroad depot in Bisbee about a pair of galoots coming in from Texas might put him on the right trail. Nothing else in the man's pockets gave a hint as to his identity.

Slocum stood and stared at the body.

"I cheated the coyotes out of Lily's body. They can feast on yours. I hope they don't choke." Slocum restrained the impulse to kick the dead man, then stripped off the dead man's gun belt, shoved the fallen six-shooter into the holster, and slung it over his shoulder.

Slocum prepared his horse, saddled, and rode after the second would-be killer. About all he could tell from the trail was that the man made a beeline toward Bisbee. Content with this for the moment, Slocum let his mare set its own pace back toward the dusty copper mining town. His quarry would tucker out his horse soon enough at the frantic pace he set. When the killer's horse balked or died under him, then he would be easy pickings for Slocum.

Slocum had figured right about the man and the way he had mistreated his horse. Fear had driven him to push the horse beyond the limits of its endurance. Slocum spotted the man walking his horse off the road less than an hour after leaving the watering hole. Reaching down, Slocum drew his Winchester from the saddle sheath and levered a round into the chamber. The metallic click as the shell seated itself brought the distant man around in sheer panic.

Slocum lifted the rifle and judged the distance. In the dark, at this range, he wasn't likely to hit anything but the man's horse. He lowered his rifle and picked up the pace to close the gap between them.

"You can't get away," Slocum shouted. "Give up and I might let you live to stand trial." This produced the kind of response he had expected. The man began firing wildly with his six-shooter. If Slocum wasn't able to hit the man with a rifle, there was no hope at all of the man getting a slug close to Slocum using a handgun. Slocum kept riding steadily, soothing his horse now and then with pats to the neck to keep it moving into the gunfire. Let the varmint expend all his ammo. That made life easier for Slocum.

And death all the more certain for the back-shooting son of a bitch he was after.

Again a turn of fate changed Slocum's tactics. The man simply vanished from sight. He and his horse were on a ridge one minute and then gone the next. When Slocum rounded the low rise after following its base, knowing better than to silhouette himself against the night sky with its bright stars, he was surprised to find a deep arroyo leading off toward a low range of mountains. The man had to be killing his horse by inches to gallop along this sandy-bottomed ravine, but that's what he did.

Slocum walked his horse along, every sense sharp. Within a mile he spotted the outlaw's dead horse. Swinging up his rifle, he looked around for a good target. Without even knowing he had found the man, Slocum drew back on the trigger and loosed a round that kicked up a dust cloud in front of a knee-high green rabbit brush. This flushed his quarry.

"Freeze or I'll drop you, I swear," Slocum called. The man took a few more staggering steps, then threw up his hands, still facing away from Slocum.

"You can't shoot a man in the back," the outlaw called. "I'm givin' up."

"Why the hell shouldn't I shoot you in the back? You shot a naked woman to death in her sleep."

"That wasn't me. I didn't do it. We was paid, but I didn't do that. It—"

The shot snapped the man's head back. He fell as if every bone in his body had turned to water. Slocum stared at his rifle, wondering if it had somehow discharged accidentally. His finger still rested on the trigger, and no recoil had pushed the rifle butt back into his shoulder.

Someone else had gunned down his only source of information. Slocum cursed and put his heels to his mare's flanks, getting the horse down the treacherous bank and into the arroyo. It was dangerous to approach the fallen man, but he had no alternative. Slocum jumped to the ground and saw the deadly bullet had caught his captive smack in the middle of the face. A quick search of the man's pockets turned up a few more greenbacks and nothing else. Not even a train ticket stub.

Slocum stripped off the man's gun belt and added it to his collection. Then he mounted and headed along the arroyo, going straight into the muzzle of the rifle that had robbed him of any chance of finding out who had killed Lily.

In the distance he heard the crunch of a horse walking across the gravelly arroyo bottom. Slocum rushed forward, his rifle swinging from side to side to cover any possible ambush. He clambered to the rim of the arroyo and caught sight of a distant, shadow-shrouded rider ducking low, then vanishing under an overhanging cottonwood limb. Slocum was robbed of a good shot. He heaved a sigh and lowered his rifle, then frowned.

Slocum inhaled deeply, trying to figure out what odor was mixed with the creosote bush and heavy sage that permeated the air. Then he shook his head and went back up the arroyo to fetch his horse. If he wanted to track down the killer of the killer, he had to get on the trail fast.

As good as he was, Slocum lost the rider he trailed within a mile.

3

Slocum rode slowly into Bisbee at midday, still fuming that he had lost the trail so quickly. The canyons and valleys around Bisbee formed a regular rat's nest that allowed anyone to disappear fast if he took it into his head to do so. Slocum was a good tracker, one of the best, and yet he had been thrown off the track because of the rocky ground interspersed with sunbaked patches harder than rock. The tall, sheer cliffs were dotted with deep holes where miners had drilled and blasted inward, hunting for blue dirt. For all Slocum knew, they might have found it. He certainly hadn't hit pay dirt in his hunt.

As the townspeople came out to peer at the stranger riding into their midst, Slocum scrutinized each and every one, driving some back inside their adobe hovels with the intensity of his hawklike stare. Any one of them might be the man he sought. But which one? Slocum had never gotten a good look because of darkness and distance. The killer was one hell of a good shot to cut down the owlhoot Slocum had captured. It had been a long, hard shot made from horseback. The killer was an expert trailsman, rode like the wind, and vanished like a ghost. For all the skill shown, the man might be an Indian, but Slocum's gut told him that wasn't so.

His gut also told him he was missing something very

important and couldn't figure out what it was. That made him even angrier as he reined back and dismounted in front of the sheriff's office.

He stood facing the door for a few seconds, but made no move to open it, go in, and report what had happened. Slocum reached back and took the pair of six-shooters he had carried since the outlaws had died and hung them over the hitching rail in front of the lawman's office. Let the worthless sheriff make of them what he might. Slocum wasn't wasting any more time bandying words with the son of a bitch just because he had a badge pinned on his shabby vest.

Taking his horse's reins, Slocum walked back down the main street and looked from one gin mill to the other, trying to decide which would give him the best drink for the cheapest price. Since Bisbee was a mining town—a boom-town, even—he had little chance of finding that particular corner of El Dorado.

Settling on Saloon No. 19 for no good reason other than it was close, Slocum went in to wet his whistle and to think about what he wanted to do next. Lily was dead, and he was no closer to bringing the murderer to justice.

"Beer," Slocum growled. He turned and spat into a brass cuspidor at the corner of the bar. The gob setting the pot to ringing was more dust than spit. He had been on the trail too long without stopping for food or water.

"Buy a second and . . ." The barkeep's voice faded away as Slocum drained the mug in one long gulp and sat it back onto the bar with a loud click.

"Another," Slocum ordered, "and what comes with it?"

"Free lunch with the second one," the barkeep finished. "Reckon you done met all the ree-quire-ments for that. That is, when you fork over a dime for the beers."

Slocum fished around in his shirt pocket and found a coin, dropping it with a silver ring to the bar. Barely had the coin stopped spinning when the barkeep neatly snared it and cached it in his beer-stained canvas apron pocket. With practiced ease, the young bartender pulled out a plate already loaded with a thick sandwich. Slocum didn't even much care that some roaches had beat him to the tastier parts. The pile of stale bread and tough meat was about the prettiest thing he had seen in a spell. It was especially tasty with enough eye-wateringly potent horseradish slathered all over it.

Slocum lit into the sandwich, but paused in his contented chewing like a cow with its cud when he looked up into the long mirror behind the bar and saw the reflection of a woman seated across the room eyeing him. He had seen hungry wolves look at lambs with less intent. The instant she saw that he had noticed her, she rose with lithe grace and sidled across the room, parading for just him.

There was a lot to parade, too. She was tallish, maybe five-foot-six, slender, but curvy in all the places where it mattered, with brunette hair done up nicely and devilish violet eyes. She wore a low-necked dress of bright red satin that revealed even more of her charms as she bent over next to Slocum. Her voice was soft, an intimate whisper only he could hear.

"Haven't seen you here before," she said. Those strange, piercing violet eyes fixed on him like daggers through his soul. Slocum kept eating. "Should I have said, haven't seen enough of you? Here?"

"Say what you please," Slocum said, finishing the rest of his sandwich and washing it down with a healthy gulp of beer. He considered ordering another beer and another sandwich. It had been way too long since he'd eaten not to appreciate the beef and bread burning with the horseradish to help it all go down smooth.

"My name's Cara. What do they call you?" She moved a little closer, her bare arm brushing against his.

"Don't want to be unfriendly," Slocum said, "but that's the arm I intend to use for lifting another mug of beer." He signaled the barkeep, who quickly drew a third glass for him.

"And the other arm," Cara said, looking around to his right hand. "That's your gun hand. I can tell you know how to use that piece of iron at your hip."

Slocum saw no reason to respond, and drank slowly now, savoring the beer and noting that it wasn't bitter like most served in Arizona. It was also cool, telling him Bisbee imported ice from somewhere with year-round ice, maybe the Sangre de Cristo Mountains in New Mexico.

"And I suspect you're right good using your . . . third arm." Cara moved even closer now, her hip rubbing seductively against his. Tiny clouds of dust rose from his clothing, getting her fancy red dress dirty. Unlike most saloon girls, Cara took no notice.

"Not interested," Slocum said.

"In what?"

"I can't meet your price," he said.

"But you *are* interested? I'd be devastated if you weren't attracted to me."

"Why's that? You have a town full of miners. Some of them would give 'bout every ounce of gold they clawed from the ground to be with a lady as pretty as you."

"My, aren't we quick with the compliments? You are both romantic and handsome," Cara said.

"Never thought of myself that way," Slocum said. He felt the woman rub against him again. He continued to drink slowly, studying her in the mirror rather than looking directly at her. This gave him a better view of the rest of the saloon, if she worked with an owlhoot to cut him from the herd and rob him. Slocum hoped it wasn't so, but Cara had taken to him too fast.

Her attraction was even less understandable when he saw a poker game in progress at the rear of the saloon. The five men at the table were well-dressed—better than Slocum would ever be—and had a small fortune piled on the table in front of them. Two looked to be tinhorn gamblers, but the other three were something more. One might be a successful miner or more likely a mine owner. The remaining two were railroad men.

Almost as if they'd heard his thoughts, a steam whistle rang out loud and clear to fill the quiet town with the raucous warning of an approaching locomotive. The two grabbed their chips, tucked them into coat pockets, and hurried from the saloon. Slocum guessed that between them they carried five hundred dollars. The three remaining at the table were still looking at a pot amounting to a hundred dollars or more. The railroad men or the remaining gamblers and the miner were all better targets for an ambitious Cyprian like Cara.

But she hadn't batted an eyelash in the other men's direction. Her attention focused entirely on John Slocum. That made Slocum even more suspicious of her intentions.

"I'd buy you a drink," Slocum said, testing the limits of her interest in him, "but all I got left is a nickel."

"A beer for me, Charlie," she called to the barkeep. The young man grinned foolishly, telling Slocum Cara had him wrapped around her little finger.

The relationship became even stranger when the barkeep set it in front of her and said, "On the house."

Slocum had never seen a bartender stand a drink for anyone, even a woman he was sweet on.

"How long you intending to be around?" Cara asked. "I hope it's a long time."

"So you can make it long?"

Cara recoiled slightly at a suggestion that should never have startled her, then laughed. "You have quite the sense of humor, don't you? I never caught your name."

"Reckon you didn't, Miss Cara," Slocum said.

Slocum finished his beer, and wondered if Cara would inveigle the barkeep to give them two more free drinks. The thought rattled around in Cara's scheming brain, he knew, but he said little and let the young barkeep pitch a little woo in her direction. The man's compliments kept interrupting hers for Slocum, until she finally gave up. But she did not stalk off or appear in the least angry that Slocum had rejected her advances at every turn. Given ordinary circumstances, Slocum might have been interested, but too much didn't add up about the woman.

And it had hardly been twenty-four hours since he had buried Lily Montrechet. Her memory still burned vivid and bright—and the need for revenge was even more intense.

"Lily," he said quietly. He shook his head as he remembered her, but how little he really knew of the woman who had been murdered sleeping next to him and whom he had buried out on the Arizona desert. Slocum wasn't even sure that Lily Montrechet was her real name. It probably wasn't, but it was all she had ever given him. She must have family somewhere, but he could never tell them how she had died—or even that she had died, because he knew nothing of where she had been born, raised, or called home.

More likely, like Slocum himself, the sky was the roof and the horizons were the walls with no town claiming her allegiance.

"What's that?" Cara moved a little closer and peered up at him, her violet eyes as intense as the noonday sun.

"Just reminiscing," Slocum said.

"Old loves? Why not come with me and find a new one? Might be I'm even better. Find out!"

Slocum saw how this bothered the barkeep. Slocum motioned for the man to come over and said, "I've got serious drinking to do. Pour me a shot of whiskey. I intend to get walleyed before I leave here."

"Sure thing, mister," the barkeep said, relieved that Cara had failed to entice him more than the lure of whiskey had. Slocum wasn't sure what the young man thought of anyone turning down such a blatant invitation from the lovely brunette Cara, but he wasn't as interested in that as what the woman would do if it appeared that he was settling in for a good, long drinking bout.

"You keep pourin' this gent whatever he wants, Charlie," Cara said. "You catch my drift?"

"Sure thing, Cara. I understand."

Slocum suspected that his drinks would be larger than usually poured and maybe of better quality, to keep him happy and drinking and away from the brunette. As he sipped at the first shot, then nodded agreeably, he knew this was exactly what was going to happen. He knocked back the round and let it slide all smooth and warm to his belly.

"Don't go wandering off now, you hear?" Cara put her hand warmly on Slocum's arm, then stepped away. Slocum watched her go in the mirror as Charlie poured another round. Slocum left it on the bar, untouched, and turned to see Cara hurry out the swinging doors leading to Bisbee's main street.

"Mister, you, uh, you—" Charlie looked distraught when he thought Slocum was going to take Cara up on her offer.

"Save my place at the bar," Slocum said. "I got to take a leak. Out back?"

"Yeah, sure, there's an outhouse back there someplace. You can't miss it,'specially if you're downwind."

"Might just piss against the back wall," Slocum said, trying to irritate the man so he would be willing to see him out of the saloon fast. The barkeep bristled a mite, then shrugged. Anything was all right with him as long as Cara went in one direction and he in the other. Slocum went to the back door without seeming to hurry. Once he was outside he ran around the saloon and peered into the street in time to see Cara duck down an alley a couple blocks away.

Slocum crossed the street and estimated how long it might take the woman, hurrying as she was, to reach the back of the buildings. He took a quick peek around and saw her talking to another woman, whose back was to Slocum. From this distance Slocum couldn't hear what was said, but Cara obviously had displeased the woman from the gestures and the obvious dressing-down she got.

As suddenly as the argument had started, it was over. Cara nodded once, her brown hair flying from the careful coiffure, then vanished back toward Bisbee's main street, probably returning to Saloon No. 19. Slocum had other ideas. He wanted a better look at the woman who had received Cara's report. As the woman hurried off, lifting her skirts enough to keep from kicking up dust as she walked,

Slocum trailed her. As he passed the spot where she and
Cara had stood, Slocum caught the faint whiff of perfume.

He tried to place the familiar scent, but couldn't. It was
a mere zephyr, tantalizing and faint to the point of hardly
existing. But it was distinctive, and made him wonder why
he couldn't place where he had smelled it before. Maybe it
had been similar to a perfume Lily had used, or one of the
members of the dance troupe at the Gala in Tombstone. He
pushed this from his mind when the woman abruptly left
the alley and headed away from the main street going directly across the desert toward the train depot.

Another screech from a train whistle sounded. Slocum
broke into a run to catch up. He didn't want the woman
getting on a train and disappearing, although finding where
she headed would be interesting. Right now Slocum
wanted something more than mere diversion to chew on.
He might be headed away from finding who had murdered
Lily, but Cara and this woman gave his only chance to discover what was going on in Bisbee.

Slocum lost sight of the woman as she climbed the steps
onto the depot platform. A chuffing engine sat at the station
house, filling the clear Arizona sky with billows of white
steam and black soot. Slocum rounded the depot and
stopped dead in his tracks. The woman was gone, but three
men jumped to the platform from the first passenger car.
From the way they wore their six-shooters low on their
hips, they were gunslingers come to Bisbee for serious
business. Lead-slinging business.

Two stepped back as the third gunman picked up his
valise, and Slocum saw his face fully illuminated by the
hot sun. He went cold inside because he recognized Boots
Wyman. Wyman and Slocum had tangled in Laredo a couple years back, with Wyman coming out second best. He
had taken one of Slocum's bullets in the leg and still hobbled slightly. If that weren't enough to identify him, he put
his foot up on a bench, pulled up his pants leg, and showed
off the flashy hand-tooled Mexican leather boots, buffing
off dust with a handkerchief. Wyman claimed to have

taken them off a notorious Mexican *bandido* he had killed in a gunfight, but Slocum knew he had stolen them from a cobbler in Guadalajara. That knowledge had led them to their showdown and the slug left in Wyman's leg.

If Boots Wyman saw him, he would not likely shoot Slocum where he stood. He would prefer to torture him to death.

Slocum stepped back, got the depot building between him and the three gunmen, then retraced his way to where he had tethered his patient mare. Bisbee was attracting some mighty strange—and deadly—folks. It was time for him to clear out or get caught in the middle of a gathering storm that was none of his concern.

4

Slocum climbed into the saddle and headed out of Bisbee at a trot, but the farther he rode the colder the lump that formed in his belly. He had nothing to fear from Boots Wyman. They had crossed paths before, and Slocum had come out on top. Wyman was a blowhard and wasn't nearly as fast with his six-gun as he bragged. If anything, Slocum reckoned Wyman had killed most of the men he bragged about by shooting them in the back. When they had faced each other, Slocum had seen the telltale flicker of fear in Wyman's eyes, although the gunman had tried hard to hide it. Slocum had played on the fear and had been quicker on the draw, more accurate with his shot, better than Wyman that hot, dusty summer day in Laredo.

Even if Wyman had two partners backing him up, Slocum couldn't turn and run like a frightened deer. Somebody had killed Lily and needed serious tending to. In a way, Wyman and his pack of mongrels made it easier to find Lily's killer. He knew the gunslicks had nothing to do with the murder since they had just arrived in Bisbee. That eliminated three men he otherwise would have wasted time on.

Slocum wheeled his mare around and walked back into town, passing the sheriff's office and wondering if Yarrow had any inkling what he faced. Wyman and the others had gotten off the Arizona Central Railroad train from El Paso like they had business in town. They weren't just passing through since Bisbee was on a spur off the Southern Pacific line that ran from California to El Paso and then down into San Antonio. Nobody simply stopped over here. They came to Bisbee with a purpose, and the only purpose men like Boots Wyman had was slaughter.

Their business might be something other than hunting for John Slocum, but always looking over his shoulder and worrying that Wyman had spotted him would make Slocum's job too hard. Better to face Wyman right away and get it over with. He pulled the Colt riding at his left hip and spun the cylinder, checking to be sure every chamber was loaded. Slocum usually rode with the hammer resting on an empty, but not now, not after his brush with death.

And Lily's.

Six rounds, three gunfighters. It seemed fair enough for Slocum, but he wanted to be sure. He pulled his Winchester from the saddle sheath and saw that its magazine was full, too. Only then did he turn toward the railroad depot and death. Just who might die, Slocum could not say, but he didn't intend it to be his.

Dropping to the ground, he rested the rifle in the crook of his arm as he deliberately climbed the steps to the platform. He looked around. The engine still chuffed and puffed at the platform, but otherwise the place was as deserted as a ghost town. He walked to the ticket window and peered through the filthy glass. The soot had accumulated and made it difficult to see inside, but he heard a familiar noise. Slocum rapped hard enough to rattle the pane of glass.

"Wha? What you want?" came the sleepy complaint from inside.

"Sorry to wake you, old-timer," Slocum said, peering through the only clean spot on the window at a man older than dirt dressed in a railroad uniform. "I'm looking for the three gents who got off the train about a half hour back. You know where they went?"

"Rough customers? Guns slung real low on their hips like they knew how to use 'em—and meant to?"

"They're the ones," Slocum said.

The old man hesitated, then said, "Nope. Ain't seen 'em."

Slocum placed his rifle on the window ledge and poked it under the glass just enough so the muzzle was inside the ticket agent's booth. He left it there for a moment, then drew back the hammer to cock the rifle. The sound echoed like the peal of doom.

"Look, mister, I ain't got no truck with them fellas. That's the God's honest truth."

"Not saying you do," Slocum said. "I just want to know where they went."

"Into town, that's where."

"That's not very helpful."

"It's all I know. They came on a special train, straight from El Paso. That's all I know, and they rode all by their lonesome like they owned the whole damn railroad. They don't, no, sir. It belongs to Mr. Peake. That there car, the engine, the tracks, the whole shebang."

Slocum pulled the rifle back and went to the edge of the platform, looking around for any trace of Wyman and his cronies. It wasn't much of a walk into Bisbee from here. Even a gimp like Wyman could make it in a few minutes. Slocum saw no point in questioning the ticket agent further. The man either wouldn't or couldn't give any more information. Let him go back to his snoring afternoon siesta.

Mounting, Slocum rode back into town.

He drew rein and looked up and down Bisbee's main street hunting for Wyman and his gang. Not seeing them, Slocum rode from one end of town to the other peering into saloons for any trace of the men. He got a few curious looks from miners in town early to begin their drinking bouts, but mostly the patrons ignored him. Slocum took a few minutes to ask after Boots Wyman, even describing him to a few of the bartenders, but none had seen Wyman. Or nobody was willing to admit it.

Disgusted as much at himself for thinking Wyman was a problem as at not finding the gunman, Slocum finally threw in the towel. His failure in turning up Wyman had caused him to work up a powerful thirst. Worse, the sun was dipping down in the west, plunging the boomtown into darkness so intense it was like swimming in an ink pot. The only light spilled from the wide-open saloon doors.

Giving in to circumstance, Slocum looked around for a decent saloon to quench that thirst. He considered seeing what Charlie back at Saloon No. 19 might have to offer, but decided to try a different watering hole. The more places he tried, the better his luck would be finding something he could use to identify Lily's killer.

"The Cat's Eye Cantina," he said, looking up at the poorly painted sign above the doorway leading into an adobe building. The crude drawing amused him. Slocum left his horse outside, silently promising the mare he would see it fed and watered soon. Then he went into the saloon, took a moment to look around the low-ceilinged room, and finally crossed to the bar.

"Beer," he ordered. The barkeep was a Mexican with a long, pink scar running across his left cheek that give him a ferocious expression. A handlebar mustache and piercing dark eyes made Slocum wonder if the bartender was a *bandido* come to rob the bar rather than to serve customers.

Without a word, the barkeep drew a mug of beer and put it in front of Slocum.

"You see a gent with fancy boots come in this afternoon?" Slocum asked.

"I don't ever see nuthin' 'cept the dime for that *cerveza*, Señor."

Slocum dropped the payment onto the stained wood surface, then sipped at the warm beer. The other saloon was not only cheaper, but had better beer. Still, Slocum decided to stay and watch the customers here for a while. The Cat's Eye catered to a completely different clientele from their look. Saloon No. 19 had high-class gamblers and mine owners at its gambling tables and bellied up to its bar.

This saloon probably required the barkeep to use the six-gun thrust into his belt to collect payment for anything more expensive than the dime beer.

Slocum quickly found that no one came to talk to him, even the drunks trying to hold themselves upright at the far end of the bar. Some silent communication had passed through the Cat's Eye making them keep away from him. He knew some Spanish and picked up snippets of conversation, but nothing that told him more than he already knew about Bisbee. Sheriff Yarrow wasn't respected or well liked, but that hardly came as a surprise. Almost finished with his beer and ready to move on to see what other saloons might have to offer, Slocum looked up and saw Cara standing in the doorway.

The low buzz in the saloon faded to nothing as all eyes turned to her. From that alone Slocum knew this wasn't her usual hangout. If he needed any further confirmation, it came when she pushed through the men between her and Slocum and came right for him.

"I wondered where you'd got off to," she said. "You want some company?"

"*I* do," piped up a drunk wedged between the bar and the dusty adobe wall. "I got money!"

Cara never glanced in his direction. Her bright violet eyes fixed unwaveringly on Slocum. In a good night, she could have had every man in the saloon for double what they usually paid for a woman. But she paid them no heed.

"You following me?" Slocum asked.

"I surely must be since I don't usually stop in here," Cara said boldly. "I go after what I want."

"You want a drink?" asked Slocum, to see how far he could push her before she said something she didn't intend saying.

"I want you, John."

"How is it that you know my name? I don't remember telling you," he said.

"Your memory might be failing you, but I doubt other parts of you would disappoint me." She sidled close. The brunette's hand pressed into his dusty shirt and worked slowly lower, stopping only when she reached the buckle of his gun belt. Once there, those long, knowing fingers drummed out a seductive rhythm that made Slocum reverberate from head to toe.

A dozen things raced through his mind, and he ignored them all.

"Not had any complaints in that department," Slocum said.

"I'm from Missouri," Cara said. "You'll have to show me."

He doubted she had ever been in Missouri, but wasn't going to argue the matter with such a deliciously willing woman. Cara had fastened herself to him like a leech back at Saloon No. 19, and must have spent the day going from one saloon to the next hunting for him when he had given her the slip. Such dedication deserved some reward.

"Here?" he asked.

"No, silly, not here." Wiggly fingers worked down under his gun belt and struggled to reach farther down. The saloon became deathly quiet as the men watched to see what would happen. Slocum decided it was time for the public show to stop—and the private one to begin.

"Let's go," he said.

"Oh?" Cara arched her carefully plucked eyebrows. "Where might we go?"

"You have a place? Or should we just tumble about in the hay out back of the stables?"

"Why not rent a room at the hotel? It's not far. You *can* make it that long, can't you?"

"You won't be disappointed at how long I can make it," Slocum said. Arm in arm, they left the Cat's Eye Saloon, turned up the main street, and walked a couple blocks before cutting to their right and heading for a three-story red-brick hotel. At first Slocum thought he had drunk a sip too much, then realized it was the hotel that was off-square and leaning precariously. A strong wind might blow it down. Or perhaps a strong wind had put it into this tilting condition. His interest in Bisbee architecture and its failings evaporated like water spilled in the hot desert when Cara spun around, came eagerly into his arms, and kissed him fervently.

"Thought you wanted a room," Slocum said when she broke off the passionate kiss.

"I do. I just couldn't wait."

"You must be in heat," Slocum said. "You see me in a saloon and ask after my name. I never told you back at the Saloon No. 19."

"Why's that so important, John? I did ask and someone told me. Not Charlie but someone else. I don't know who. But I've been hankering to climb on and ride from the second I laid eyes on you."

"They're mighty pretty eyes, too," Slocum said, staring down into those violet pools. He was startled to read the lust there. Intense lust. No soiled dove had this look if she bedded a man only for money. Slocum hesitated, wondering what really drove Cara. Then the ruminations became a distant memory as she kissed him again.

This time her agile tongue slipped from between her ruby lips and tried to intrude into his mouth. In the middle of the street, they stood oblivious to the world around them, totally wrapped up in the erotic duel of tongues and lips. Cara finally gasped and backed away, fanning herself with her hand and looking at him with mock coyness.

"I do declare, you do heat up a girl's passions."

"That's not all I can heat up, but unless you want to do it in the middle of the road, we should get ourselves into the hotel and find a nicely accommodating feather bed."

"A feather bed," Cara sighed. "So soft. And so hard." Her hand flashed out and grabbed his crotch, squeezing down until Slocum hopped about in discomfort. He reached down and caught her slender wrist, pulling her hand away so he could walk.

Together they went up the rickety hotel steps, their hips rubbing suggestively as they went.

"A room," Slocum said. The clerk looked up, his eyes fixed hard on Slocum.

"Fer the night? Or jist an hour?"

"All night," Slocum said, thinking it would startle the man. This unusual request didn't cause the man's stare to leave him and go to Cara for even a fleeting moment. Slocum thought this was passing odd since such a lovely woman, the pale white globes of her breasts almost falling out of the scoop-necked fancy red dress, ought to have attracted more than passing notice from the clerk. But she hadn't.

"Two dollars."

Slocum passed over a pair of faded, wadded-up greenbacks and watched them vanish from the counter. Replacing them came a jagged brass key fastened to a large wood block with the number 7 carved on it.

"All the way back, through there," the clerk said, pointing to the doorway half hidden by the stairs going to the upper floors.

"Come on, John. Let's hurry," Cara said.

Slocum was again aware that the clerk never glanced in her direction, even to momentarily fantasize about what he might be missing stuck behind the counter. Slocum let the woman pull him along under the stairs and down a narrow corridor to the last room on the left. He tried the key and opened the door to a small, neat room holding a bed with what looked to be clean sheets, a night table, and nothing more. But there wasn't a whale of a lot more that Slocum and Cara needed.

"Nice," Slocum said.

"You mean the room or me? If you mean me, you've got a surprise in store. There's nothing nice about me. I'm wild as the West Texas wind when I get into bed with the right man!" Cara danced into the room, kicked the door shut with her heel, and used the key to lock them in. With the door shut, the room plunged into darkness. It took Slocum's eyes a few seconds to adjust. Then he saw starlight filtering in through a high window in the wall and casting a silvery glow on the bed.

"I can't wait to see what I've been missing," Cara said, beginning to strip off her dress.

"Wait," Slocum said, coming around to face her. "We do this my way."

"What's that?" she asked suspiciously.

"We take our time. We got all night," he said.

"I knew I had found me a good one," Cara said ecstatically. "What do you want me to do?"

"Lie back on the bed and close your eyes. Don't open them, no matter what."

"You could blindfold me," she suggested.

"Don't want to tear up the sheet," Slocum said. "Now do it." A sharp snap of command came to his voice, the tone he had used while he had been an officer in the CSA.

Cara flopped back on the bed, her legs dangling down over the side. "Can I talk or should I stay quiet?"

"I don't like my women to stay quiet. I like to hear the moans," Slocum said. He ran his hand under her skirt and slowly worked his way up her leg, feeling the muscles tense as he stroked toward her crotch. Slocum delighted in the sleek flow of her smooth skin, hidden away under the voluminous skirt and only slowly coming to be illuminated by the stars.

A light kiss here and there followed by quick, catlike licks made Cara shiver all over. Then the brunette lifted her knees and scooted the fabric of her dress back so Slocum could have untrammeled access to the spot they both sought to fill.

Slocum rummaged about at the night table, prompting Cara to sit up.

"No peeking," he said sternly.

"What're you doing?"

"Getting rid of my gun belt," he said, dropping it on the floor. "Now, none of this back talk."

"I—" Cara gasped as Slocum returned his attentions to her bare legs, stroking until he came to the rounded half-moons of her buttocks. His strong fingers squeezed down, and then he grabbed a double handful of womanly flesh and began massaging gently. The woman melted on the bed, moaning softly as she writhed about. The brunette arched her back when his finger found a tight hole to penetrate, but as quickly as he dipped in, he retreated.

"Most women wear frilly undergarments. You don't," he said.

"All the better for you to—oh!"

He gave her no time for a smart answer. His hand moved steadily up inside her thigh until his thumb found the soft fleshy curtains protecting her inner fastness. His thumb sank deeply into her moist interior and began moving about slowly. He gripped firmly and held his position as she thrashed about in growing ardor at his gentle invasion.

While his thumb diddled her, he used his other hand to push away the unwanted curtain of her bodice. Her melon-shaped breasts popped out, then bounced delightfully as Cara began struggling on the bed. Slocum bent low and lightly kissed first one and then the other nipple questing upward, hard and pulsing with blood from her frenzied heart. Then he sucked hard and took as much of that pillowy mound into his mouth as he could.

His teeth raked the slopes, and his tongue shoved out hard against the rock-hard pebble capping the breast. He tried to ram the throbbing button of red flesh all the way down into the pliable underpinning. The combination of his oral assault and the way his thumb worked down lower set off the woman.

Cara cried out in joy, clamped her legs together hard, and almost flopped off the bed in the throes of her sexual release. Panting, she settled down, only to find Slocum still working at her most sensitive areas. His lips brushed across her cheek as he went to nibble at her ear. His hand, the one not working so assiduously at her womanly center, cupped a snowy breast and crushed it. With her nipple between thumb and forefinger, he squeezed down hard, rolled it around, and then pulled.

Cara cried out again.

"I'm so weak, John. I feel weak and watery inside. I never felt like this with a man before. Oh, please, don't stop. I want more. I want this!"

She grabbed for his leg, worked, and found that he had unbuttoned his jeans. The sex-hungry brunette reached into his fly and caught at the fleshy pillar standing hard and tall and proud there. She tugged insistently, pulling him between her widespread legs and into position.

"Yes, John, now, do it now." Cara raised her knees and then gasped as Slocum smoothly slipped forward, unerringly finding the spot in the fleecy nut-colored love nest that was his target. For a moment, he paused, the arrowhead tip of his organ parting her nether lips. Then he slid inward, sinking deeply.

Surrounded by her clinging, clutching warm tunnel, Slocum groaned with the stark pleasure of it. He relished the tightness and the heat boiling within the aroused woman's body. Then she began tensing and relaxing her knowing inner muscles in an attempt to milk him of his resolve. Slocum resisted for a moment, enjoying the sensations jolting into his loins, then withdrew slowly.

"No, no," she pleaded. "In me. I have to have it in all the waaay!"

Slocum gave the sultry woman her wish and slammed forward, their groins grinding together in a circular motion. He corkscrewed in and out, twisting and turning and rotating his hips in a broad circle that stirred Cara's passions to the breaking point. Slocum heard her gulp; then a slow tide of climax rolled through her, taking him with it.

He tried to resist the irresistible and could not. He began pumping furiously, trying to burn them both up with the carnal friction of his movement. He arched his back in an attempt to split her supple, clutching body in half. It failed, but the reward was immense, anyway. He spilled his seed, and Cara cried out for a final time.

Spent, Slocum sagged down to the bed. He had intended for it to last longer, but the brunette was too demanding.

Rolling onto his back, he saw her climb from the bed. It was as if a white marble statue had come alive, moving to the night table beside the bed.

"What are you doing?" Slocum asked. He enjoyed the play of her muscles, the bounce of her teats, the way starlight cast dark shadows and gleaming silvery streaks over her body.

"I'm getting something from the drawer, John. I must say, you are a source of constant amazement."

Cara stepped back and lifted the derringer in a steady hand.

"You're pretty amazing yourself," Slocum said, his eyes on the small two-shot pistol.

"I wish it could be different, but I must kill you now." Cara laughed joyously. "You're the first man I've truly savored in a long, long time and I must kill you."

"Why?" asked Slocum. "Are you some kind of black widow spider? Or was it something I did?"

"You did everything wondrously well, my dear John. I regret having to do this sorry deed, but I must. I will."

Bathed in the faint starlight, Cara lifted the derringer, cocked it, aimed between Slocum's eyes, and pulled the trigger.

5

The dull click of the hammer falling on an empty chamber was drowned out by Cara's curse. A second click followed quickly as she tried the other chamber. Slocum sat up in bed and looked at her, so pale and lovely and bare—and furious that she had failed to kill him in the bed where they'd just made love.

"I took these out," Slocum said, reaching down under the pillow and holding two cartridges in the palm of his hand. "I'd wondered why the clerk shuttled us to this particular room. He was acting strange, so I decided to see what was in the night table. Lucky for me I found the derringer and unloaded it. Why do you want to kill me?"

Cara let out an incoherent cry and threw the useless derringer at Slocum. He ducked to one side, then saw she hadn't intended it to do him any harm. All she wanted was to make him duck so she could escape. He saw her naked body flash whitely as she opened the door and light from the oil lamps in the hallway bathed her. Then she was gone. He heard her bare feet padding swiftly down the hall.

Slocum rolled from bed and climbed into his clothes as fast as he could. He tucked the two shells from Cara's derringer into his pocket along with her empty weapon, then jerked on his boots and lit out after her. He didn't think there would be much trouble following her. All he had to do was look for the sea of miners, heads turned in the direction Cara had run. Even in a town like Bisbee, an unclad woman running through the streets had to attract some attention.

Ducking, he got through the door from under the stairs and went into the lobby. The clerk sat behind the counter, his jaw open.

"She . . . she's not got no clothes on."

Slocum laughed harshly. "I misjudged you. I thought you were dead below the waist as well as between the ears. Now I know for certain you're in cahoots with her." Slocum drew his six-shooter and pointed it at the man's face. "Why'd she want me dead?"

"I dunno, mister. Honest. I never laid eyes on her 'fore this afternoon. She came and told me to give you that room when you and her came in. The one in the back, outta the way, nobody on this floor. She poked around in there a spell 'fore she decided on it. Looked at all the rooms, she did. I don't even know her name!"

Slocum considered the clerk's response, then stuffed his six-gun back into the cross-draw holster, strapped it around his waist as he left the hotel, and stepped into the cold desert night. He shivered. Cara would be running along dressed in nothing more than gooseflesh. There was no good reason for her to have tried to kill him as she had. For whatever reason, the brunette had gone to a lot of trouble to find out his name and then seduce him so she could kill him in relative privacy.

Slocum frowned as he walked along, hunting for a sign the woman had come this way. There were too many things that didn't add up. He would have bet money no one in town knew his name, except Boots Wyman, and the gunman hadn't shown up until after Cara had tried to cozy up at the Saloon No. 19. The mystery intensified. Somebody had deliberately killed Lily. Of that Slocum was certain since a second shot would have taken him out, also. But tracking down the actress's killer was proving stranger—and harder—than he had anticipated.

One thing was certain. There was a long string of dead bodies behind him, and he had barely avoided joining that gruesome company of corpses.

Standing in the middle of the main street, Slocum looked up and down and knew instantly which way to go. In front of a saloon a block away stood a tight knot of miners, all chattering like magpies and pointing. Slocum sauntered down and tapped one grizzled miner on the shoulder.

"Which way'd she go?" he asked.

"You seen her, too? Then we're not all drunker 'n lords and imaginin' it. I thought I seen a pink elly-phant once when I got soused, but never seen nuthin' like *her*!" The miner pointed down a side street leading to the next block of businesses. From the way the miners stood clumped together, Slocum wondered what more had happened. He asked.

"She was nekkid as a jaybird, she was. Then that fella, the one with the big smoke wagon danglin' at his hip, he come up and gave her his coat. They went off t'gether. That way. Down toward the red-light district."

Slocum dashed in the direction of the miner's stare, turned a corner, and was in a different world. The lights had blazed brightly along Bisbee's main street, but not here. Darkness was interrupted only by an occasional kerosene lamp shining through a dirty glass window in the rows of dingy cribs. A few doorways held partially clad women hawking their wares, but otherwise the street was deserted.

He walked slowly now, looking all around. He saw a white flash from the corner of his eye, turned, and spotted Cara. She hunkered down behind a water barrel. The instant their eyes locked, green on violet, she rose and bolted, her fine rounded buttocks all Slocum could see under the long coat around her shoulders until she turned the corner of the building and raced off into the night.

He lit out after her, his stride long and his determination to catch her great. Cara held the answers to a lot of vexing questions. He doubted she knew anything about Lily's death, but as mixed up as everything was, he couldn't discount that until he had spoken to Cara at length.

Slocum closed the distance between them, no matter how Cara tried to dodge and duck. He reached out, his fingers closing around an arm. The brunette jerked away, but Slocum had thrown her off balance and bore her to the ground. He expected to hold her down and question her, but got a surprise. She lithely twisted, doubled into a ball, and kicked out. Her bare feet caught him in the belly and shoved him back. He slammed hard into the side of a building and knocked loose a board that crashed down onto the top of his head. It smarted a little but worse, it caused him to lose his footing. He sat down hard, the splintery wood plank wall behind him.

By the time Slocum got to his feet, Cara was gone again. He took a deep breath and set out looking for her. The cold night had to be taking a toll on the naked woman's stamina, but Slocum couldn't count on just that. If Cara took refuge in any of the brothels lining the street, finding her might be impossible.

He rounded the building, went to the center of the dark street, and listened hard. He turned slowly and finally homed in on the thumping sound of bare feet against hard-packed dirt. With a deliberate stride he went after her. And found her again, but this time there was a new problem to face.

Cara stood with the coat around her bare shoulders, talking to the man who had given her the protection against the cold. Slocum recognized him as one of the gunmen who had arrived on the train with Boots Wyman.

Whether Cara and the gunfighter knew each other before coming together was another question he needed to answer. Slocum made sure his Colt Navy slipped easily in his holster, then advanced at the same rapid clip he had used following the woman to this point.

"Kill him! There he is!" cried Cara.

The gunman was a little slow to understand what she was saying. He stared at her, probably bewitched by the way his coat hung open in the front, revealing most of Cara's ample charms.

By the time the gunman figured out what was happening and went for his gun, Slocum had already cleared leather. In the dark his aim wasn't as good as it usually was, but Slocum's bullet still found a target. The gunman grunted and grabbed for his right forearm. His pistol dropped to the ground from his nerveless fingers.

"Don't go for it, or I'll kill you. I swear it," Slocum said. There was no hint of mercy in his tone. The gunman looked into Slocum's eyes and saw deadly determination.

"Kill him, you fool. He's the one!" Cara rushed over and shoved the gunman hard enough to stagger him. For an instant Slocum followed the man. This let Cara drop to her knees and heft the fallen six-shooter. She got off a shot that went high. Slocum heard it tear a hunk out of a wall somewhere behind him. Angry cries rapidly followed.

"Don't make me shoot you," Slocum said. At this range he couldn't miss.

Cara seemed not to hear. She struggled to draw back the hammer on the thumb-buster.

Slocum wasn't going to give her a second chance to shoot him. He lifted his Colt and aimed carefully. Just as his finger came back on the trigger, a heavy shoulder slammed into the middle of his back, knocking him forward. His gun discharged, and he heard Cara gasp in pain, but the woman was still able to shoot. The bullet whined past Slocum and slammed into the man who had struck him.

"You there, stop shootin'!" came the aggrieved command. "This here's the sheriff. Sheriff Yarrow! In the name of the law, stop that damned shootin'!"

Slocum stumbled along, getting his gun up to take another shot at Cara. He held off firing when he saw her doubled up on the ground, clutching her belly. His shot had caught her low in the stomach. Bare flesh turned dark with blood oozing from her gut, and her fingers were no longer capable of holding the heavy six-shooter she had picked up.

"What the hell's goin' on here?" demanded the sheriff.

He pushed Slocum's pistol to one side and tried to intimidate him with his mere presence. Slocum looked past the man to where Cara moaned and writhed, even as she curled up tighter into an agonized ball of naked flesh.

"She got shot in the gut," Slocum said.

"That gunfighter fella, the one you shot in the arm. Where'd he get off to?" asked the lawman.

Slocum shook his head. He saw that the man who had tried to tackle him was slow in getting to his feet. A bloody scratch across his cheek showed where Cara's bullet had first hit him. The half-missing ear that spurted blood told the rest of the story. Beside the wounded man stood another deputy, his badge pinned onto his vest crookedly.

"This is—" The sheriff never got any farther. Cara's wounding and the sudden appearance of the three lawmen had distracted Slocum.

"The gunman!" Slocum cried. Slocum shoved the sheriff back hard, then grabbed a handful of the lawman's vest and swung him around to get him to dubious safety behind a hitching post. Slocum kept spinning around, brought up his six-shooter, and fired to keep the gunman occupied until he presented a better target.

Slocum waited, then saw the orange tongue of flame snap out in his direction from shadows across the street. Unerringly pointing his six-gun, Slocum fired. He fired a second and then a third time until there was no return fire.

"Ya got the stinkin' bastard," said the unwounded deputy. Slocum glanced at the man and saw he hadn't bothered drawing his own hogleg. "Good shootin'."

"Is the sheriff all right?" Slocum asked.

"How about it, Sheriff Yarrow? You still in one piece?"

"Shut yer tater trap," growled Yarrow, on hands and knees. He shook all over, then got to his feet. Slocum reckoned the sheriff had a touch of arthritis from the painful way he moved. The sheriff came over and shoved his face into Slocum's. "Mighta knowed you'd be at the center of this here earthquake. What 'n hell happened?"

"He saved yer life. Mine, too, I suspect. Could be he

even kept Rolf from gettin' shot up even more 'n he already is." The uninjured deputy sounded as if this was something to give Slocum a medal for. The sheriff's ugly expression hinted that wasn't going to happen.

"Shut *up*!" Sheriff Yarrow swung around and shoved his face into the deputy's until the man backed down and fell silent. "I don't like keepin' the peace in Bisbee. They don't pay me enough to take care of the county and the damn city. They surely don't pay me near enough to put up with your guff."

"The girl," Slocum interrupted, "needs a doctor. She took a round in the belly."

"Why's she wearin' that coat? Belongs to Dumont, from the look."

"Dumont's the gunman?" Slocum tried to remember if he had ever heard the name before, especially in connection with Boots Wyman. He didn't think so.

Sheriff Yarrow ignored his question as he walked across the street and poked at the dead man's body, rolling him over with the toe of his boot. Yarrow grunted from the exertion, confirming what Slocum had seen. The sheriff was a pile of aching joints and rattling bones.

"That's him," the sheriff verified. "What's goin' on here?"

"We can hash it out after the woman's looked at by a doctor. You got one in Bisbee?"

"Over by the railroad yard." Yarrow grumbled under his breath, then shouted, "You two worthless turds. Git her on over to Doc Benbow's office. Try not to bang her up too much more 'n she already is."

"She ain't got much on, Sheriff," said Rolf, pressing his bandanna against his ruined ear. The bleeding had slowed as the blood clotted, but he looked as if he had just lost a war.

"Keep your hands to the parts that'll get her moved fastest, damn your filthy mind." Yarrow continued to grumble as the two deputies worked their hands under Cara and lifted her. The woman wasn't dead yet, but might be in a few minutes from their rough handling. Slocum said noth-

ing as he watched the deputies stagger off, the one trying to
keep his bandanna on his own wound and not doing a good
job of it.

Slocum felt nothing about Cara. She had tried to kill
him twice. As much as he wanted to find out what her beef
with him was, if she died, it mattered less to him than if his
horse had drunk too much water and bloated.

"You, what's yer name?"

Slocum looked at the sheriff and saw the lawman's
anger was building.

"John Slocum, and I was the one she tried to kill. Twice.
That gunslinger yonder," Slocum said, pointing in Dumont's direction. "What's his business in Bisbee?"

"I ask the questions," Yarrow growled. He hitched up his
gun belt, then let it settle down under his amble belly.
"Don't know why him and Wyman and that other owlhoot
blowed into town right now. And I don't know 'bout that
light-o'-love, neither. That's why yer gonna tell me,
Slocum."

Slocum pursed his lips and thought a moment. The
sheriff hadn't been interested in helping find Lily's killer,
so why had he taken an interest in Cara and Wyman and
whatever mischief they were up to? Simply because it was
under his nose? Or could Yarrow have some other reason?

"I can find out a bit more about her," Slocum said. "I
know where she left her clothes."

"Reckoned you might. Go fetch her duds and meet me
at Doc Benbow's office."

"Down by the rail yard," Slocum said.

"Don't make me come for you, boy."

Slocum kept from laughing. From all he had seen of
Sheriff Yarrow and his two deputies, they couldn't find
their own asses with both hands in less than a week. He
kept a poker face and nodded once. Then he hurried back
to the hotel, went by the room clerk without saying a word,
and entered the last room in the hall. Cara's clothing was in
a pile where she had discarded it before jumping into bed
with him.

Slocum touched his pocket and felt the outline of the two cartridges and derringer there to force him to remember how dangerous the lovely brunette had been. He didn't cotton much to shooting women, but his only regret was that the deputy had spoiled his aim. Only wounding Cara might work out for the best, he reflected as he searched through her clothes. He wanted to find whoever had murdered Lily, but didn't like looking over his shoulder all the time to see if someone was going to shoot him in the back.

The woman's clothing turned up nothing, or so he thought until his fingers raked over a spot that crinkled strangely. Working through the layers of cloth, he found a small pocket in the skirt and pulled out a railroad ticket. Slocum held it up and read the faded ink on it.

Yuma. Cara had come to Bisbee from Yuma only a day before Slocum had ridden into town. This deepened the mystery of why she had tried to kill him. It had been quite a spell since he had ridden through Yuma, and he would have remembered if he had ever seen Cara before.

Slocum bundled the clothing and left the hotel.

"Hey, mister, you gonna pay for the disturbance?" called the clerk. "Got other customers what complained 'bout the noise."

"Tell them to stuff cotton in their ears next time they stay here," Slocum said. The clerk had only tried to get a few dollars more from him. Slocum doubted anyone had complained, especially if they had caught sight of Cara running away naked. An attraction like a pretty unclad woman running around at night would have miners flocking to stay here.

Slocum stepped into the night, got his bearings, and headed for the railroad depot. His pace slowed when he saw two men ahead of him, also going toward the train still parked at a siding. At this time of night, men usually didn't go out for a constitutional. More than this, one of the men limped. Slocum tucked Cara's clothing under his left arm and drew his six-shooter in case Boots Wyman noticed anyone behind him.

Wyman and his partner made a beeline for the siding where the train with its few passenger cars sat like some giant metallic beast waiting to pounce. Slocum watched Wyman swing up into the lead car, followed closely by his partner. Slocum took a few minutes to reload his six-shooter, then followed cautiously.

A light came on inside the car, causing Slocum to freeze like a deer. He saw the outline of a man against a drawn curtain and knew Wyman and his partner were settling in for the night. He advanced and stood under the open window to eavesdrop.

"Dumont was a fool to get mixed up in a gunfight like that," Wyman said. "Any idea who killed him?"

"I heard from the stupid deputy," the other said.

"The stupid deputy?" Wyman laughed harshly. "Which one's that?"

"Both," his partner said. "But this is the one that didn't get his ear blown off. I think Dumont shot him, from what he said. Mostly he bragged 'bout how he killed a gunfighter."

"He killed Dumont?"

"Naw, no way. He was too confused about what happened to ever figure out that he should have been shooting and not standing and watching."

"We got to report to the boss," Wyman said. At this Slocum perked up. Someone had sent Wyman and his two henchmen to Bisbee for some reason that couldn't have anything to do with Slocum. They were already on their way here before the dustup in Tombstone had caused Lily and him to hightail it.

"What'll we do?"

"Who the hell knows?" Wyman ranted and raved a while longer, then said, "Turn down that light. I want to get some sleep."

The sounds from inside told Slocum this was a specially outfitted car, maybe one used by the Arizona Central Railroad's owner. How Wyman had come to use it as his personal hotel was something that might have intrigued Slocum if he hadn't been more intent on finding Lily Mon-

trechet's killer. As it stood, Wyman and his partner were
mere nuisances.

But Slocum knew he might have to deal with such nuisances, the way he had Dumont. He backed from the railcar and went to find the doctor's surgery. Cara might be
alive and able to tell him what he needed to know.

6

Slocum walked with a weary step to the road running behind the railroad depot. He hadn't any good idea where the doctor's surgery might be, but the sheriff had said it was around here somewhere. It was still a couple hours until dawn, and Slocum walked until he saw a light burning in a window. At this time of night, there was little chance anyone would be up and about, even the earliest riser. He went to the door and knocked.

To his surprise, a woman answered.

"Yes?" She looked at him with open, honest eyes, but held the door firmly, as if she thought she could slam it in his face if the need arose. The blond woman had her hair pulled back in a severe bun that did nothing to hide her beauty. Her tanned, oval face was animated, and Slocum thought her lips would be quick to smile. Something about her demeanor told him she was a friendly person.

"I'm looking for the town doctor. Benbow, I think his name is."

"You're out of luck, sir," the woman said, brushing her hair back when a strand tried to escape and fall across her jade green eyes. "Dr. Benbow is out at the Hendrickson ranch. Mr. Hendrickson fell from the loft and busted himself up pretty good."

She stepped forward and got a better look at him. Her

eyes widened for a moment, as if she recognized him. Then she visibly controlled herself and added, "If there's something I can help with, I'll see what I can do, but you don't seem to be hurt."

Slocum wondered at the way she said that. Her tone implied that she regretted the fact he wasn't all shot up or limping from a broken leg. He studied her a bit harder, wondering if they had met before. Slocum doubted it. He would have remembered anyone as lovely as this woman, and was beginning to think that every woman in Bisbee was beautiful. But then she was only the second he had seen, and Cara had made a point of tracking him down and trying to shoot him. Still, two such lovelies in a mining town had to be a record of some sort. Most ladies in such towns were ladies of the evening and uglier than a mud fence.

"Sheriff Yarrow had his deputies take a woman who'd been shot to the doctor's office. If they don't know the doc's out of town, they might just let her die."

"You don't hold the law in very high esteem, do you, sir?" Her words might have carried rebuke, but the tiny curl of her lips as she tried to hold down a smile told him she shared his opinion of Yarrow's two deputies. And that might even extend to the sheriff himself.

"These two deputies haven't shown themselves to be of very high caliber, ma'am," Slocum said. "Since this isn't the doctor's surgery, could you direct me that way? I saw the light in the window and reckoned this was the place."

"You're new in town?"

Slocum hesitated answering. Something about the woman's question put him on edge, and he couldn't put his finger on it.

"Just got into town," he said.

She nodded. For the briefest instant, her lips thinned to a razor's slash. Then she smiled.

"Who's the woman you're looking for?"

"Her name's Cara, and she was gunned down about a half hour back. If you were up reading you must have heard the gunshots."

"What makes you think I was reading?"

"Can't imagine what else you'd be doing in the middle of the night, your light on and all." For Slocum it wasn't too much of a leap of imagination. The woman was fully dressed and had fresh dust smudges on her left cheek, as if she had absently reached up and touched herself with a finger dusty from a seldom-read book. The wick in the oil lamp she held up to better see him had been trimmed recently and gave out a pure white light perfect for reading.

"I might have been with someone," she said.

"You're not wearing a wedding ring, and you don't look like a woman of easy virtue." Slocum saw the shock on her face again, and again she quickly hid it. Playing poker with her would be interesting, learning what all these false starts and facial twitches meant. He had the feeling they were conversing, but each was hearing something entirely different from what the other said.

"I suppose that was meant as a compliment. I'll take it that way, sir."

"Direct me to the doctor's office and—"

"There's no need. The reason I'm up is that the deputies brought the poor girl here. I work as a midwife and might be about the only one in this godforsaken town who could help her. She was quite seriously injured."

"She's here?" Slocum looked into the small house and thought there might be a bedroom leading off the main room.

"Do you know her name, sir?"

"Cara was about all I'd heard," he said, again walking on eggs with the woman. "With the gunfight and all, there wasn't much time to exchange names."

"Of course not. Are you a friend?"

"I was the one who shot her," Slocum said, fishing for a reaction. The blond woman covered her reaction better this time. He barely saw a flicker in those polar-blue eyes. He wished they weren't half-cloaked in shadow because of the way she held the lamp so he could get an even better look at her.

"I am sure it was an accident," she said. The woman frowned, then asked, "It was an accident, wasn't it?"

"Cara got caught in cross fire between a gunman named Dumont and me."

"What's this town coming to? Gunfights and killers and innocent women being shot. Please, sir, don't stand out there. Come in."

She stepped back and let him pass. As Slocum went by, he caught a faint whiff of her perfume. Something about it made him struggle for the proper memory, but he couldn't dredge it up. Then he was occupied with the woman as she placed the coal-oil lamp on the table and turned it up to il-luminate the entire room.

The growing illumination let him get a better look at her. She was dressed simply, but the dress was clean and, if Slocum was any judge, brand-new. She filled it out quite well, and the hand resting on the wheel that adjusted the lamp wick was a stranger to serious work. The skin was sleek, white, and unblemished by cuts, blisters, or calluses. Her fingernails were trimmed and unbroken. As she real-ized he studied her, she quickly put her hands into the folds of her skirt and turned away.

"Can I see Cara?" he asked.

"She's sleeping. Do be quiet." The woman went to the door leading to the bedroom and opened it a few inches. Slocum peered in and saw a deathly pale Cara on the bed. Her breathing was ragged, and she looked closer to death than life.

"Is she going to make it?"

"You inflicted a terrible wound, sir. The slug went com-pletely through her, which is good since I lack the skill to dig it out. But I'm not sure as to the extent of her internal injuries. If you nicked her intestines, there's not a great deal I can do other than watch her die. By morning we'll know if she's going to live."

"Almost dawn," Slocum observed.

"Perhaps that was an exaggeration, then," the blonde said. She closed the door, shutting off Slocum's view of the sleeping woman. It was just as well since Slocum wanted to go to Cara and shake the information from her. She was alive only because the deputy had rammed into him. Slocum felt no chivalry whatsoever toward a woman who had tried to gun him down twice in one evening, even if she had tried to kill him somewhat more pleasurably earlier. He wondered if anyone had ever died of too much lovemaking. It would have been fun trying to find out with Cara.

Or the blonde who maneuvered herself to keep her face in shadows as she moved about the room.

"You seem distracted," the blond woman said, half-turning to look over her shoulder at him.

"Sorry, just reminiscing a mite," Slocum said. He introduced himself, watching carefully for a reaction.

"Pleased to make your acquaintance, Mr. Slocum," she said. "I'm Belle Wilson."

"Miss Wilson," he said, politely touching the brim of his hat. He had been so engrossed in finding Cara that he had neglected to remove it when he had entered the house. Slocum removed his hat and held it in his hands, wondering if he ought to drop it somewhere. Looking around, he wondered at what the woman had been up when he had knocked on the door. Dust lay thick all around. She hadn't been cleaning and he saw no open book to show she had been seated in the only chair reading. Also, the table holding the lamp was a bit far away for her to do any close work while seated in the chair. Slocum wasn't sure any of his observations meant anything because he was as jumpy as a raw nerve in a tooth after the gunplay earlier—and Cara's bold attempt to ventilate him the way she had.

"You look plumb tuckered out, Mr. Slocum," she said. "Can I fix you a cup of coffee?"

"That'd be too much trouble," Slocum said, but he hoped she would insist. She did. He took a seat in the solitary chair to one side of the main room while she went to a Franklin stove, poked up the fire, and then hunted for coffee, going through one cabinet after another.

"I do declare, I need to get to the store more often."

Slocum wondered that she had missed the small, familiar bag in one cabinet, but said nothing. Belle found it on a second search, poured the ground coffee into a strainer, and put the coffeepot on the stove top. Only when it was heating did she look around, see a chair at the table, and drag it over to sit facing Slocum.

"You must feel terrible about shooting that poor girl," Belle said, hands folded in her lap and staring at him with wide blue eyes.

"Not much has gone right since I got to Bisbee," Slocum admitted.

"Where did you ride in from?"

"What makes you think I rode? I could have taken the train."

Belle laughed and shook her head. "Oh, no, not the train. It makes too few stops here. This is a spur line, not on the main line. The Arizona Central Railroad sets its own schedule coming to Bisbee, and that usually means a load of copper ore is going out or the railroad's owner is coming to town."

"Why would a railroad magnate come here?" asked Slocum. "This can't be the most important stop along the road."

"It's not. Mr. Peake is quite conscientious about making certain every depot, every inch of track, every piece of rolling stock is in perfect condition. Bisbee is the newest of the spur lines, so he comes here often to check business. I believe he is also friends with Judge Bisbee." She saw his expression. "Judge DeWitt Bisbee is financial backer of the Copper Queen Mine, the reason this town was founded. Since then, gold has been discovered east of here."

"Peake owns a mine or two? Is that it?" Slocum doubted mere friendship would bring a wealthy railroad owner here. Rather, Judge Bisbee would travel to a bigger city where he could spend his money and lord it over the more impoverished citizens.

"Why, I think that might be the case. I've never heard,"

Belle said. She looked at Slocum more closely. "You're not what I expected."

"How could you have expected anything from me?"

Belle opened her mouth, then clamped it shut, as if she had been caught in a lie. She took a deep breath, giving him a delightful view of her crisply encased breasts rising and falling.

"I meant that you have an outlook on business and the world that is different from what I expect of a drifter."

"There's a powerful lot of time to ride and think on things," Slocum said.

"And what do you think about, Mr. Slocum, when you're alone out in the desert, riding from town to town? A woman, perhaps?"

Slocum was relaxing, his body finally demanding some rest. He worked to keep his eyes open as he sat in the comfortable chair in Belle Wilson's front room. Almost before he realized it, he was telling her about Lily Montrechet and how she had died in the desert.

"That's terrible, John," Belle said. "You and this actress had come from Tombstone?" She frowned, as if this didn't set right with her.

"Let's just say the ruckus in Tombstone was enough for us to ride out as fast as we could. I never saw anything like it. Lily was singing up there on the stage when those two owlhoots started shooting up the theater. They were aiming for her, too."

"Everyone's a critic," Belle said, smiling. Slocum saw nothing funny in that.

"We hightailed it from Tombstone heading here because Lily had a friend who might have helped her. We camped near a watering hole and that's where she was killed. A single shot."

"You are so lucky you weren't similarly murdered," Belle said.

"They wanted Lily dead, not me. I don't understand why."

"Some jealous lover, perhaps?"

"Why not kill me, too?" Slocum felt his eyelids drooping again. "Mind if I get that cup of coffee now? I'm half-asleep. Sorry, too, since you're such good company."

"I bet you say that to all the ladies," Belle said, chuckling.

"No, not really. Most aren't. Real ladies, that is."

Slocum took the coffee and drank it. Belle wasn't much for fixing tasty coffee, but he didn't care. It was hot and kept him awake. For a few minutes. They continued talking, and he felt his head bobbing about.

He came awake once to find Belle standing in front of him. Out of sheer reflex, he had his six-shooter out and pointed at her.

"Sorry," he said, "you shouldn't sneak up on me like that."

"You're very quick with that iron," she said. "I hadn't expected that. You're a surprising man, John."

"How's Cara doing?" he asked. Slocum wanted to get what information he could from the brunette so he could get on with his search for Lily's killer. Then he could leave all the craziness he had found in Bisbee far behind, hidden by his dust cloud as he rode to somewhere friendlier.

"I'll check," Belle said, moving out of his line of sight. He didn't replace the six-gun, but laid it across his lap, keeping his hand on it. As tired as he was, Slocum didn't trust himself to be able to draw it again should the need arise.

Half-asleep, he wondered why he thought that it might be necessary to do some more shooting. Belle was a likable, caring woman. He was safer here in her house than he ever would be in a hotel. Slocum drifted off to sleep again, thoughts jumbling in his head.

A scraping sound brought him back from the muzzy arms of Morpheus. He realized he had not gone completely to sleep by the way his hand felt wrapped around the ebony butt of his Colt. It wasn't cramped, and he had no sensation of time having passed. It was still dark outside, but faint traces of light worked their way into the small house through the doorway.

This brought him bolt upright, pistol pointed in that direction. The door stood open. Slocum got to his feet and
went over. The sound of it grating against the jamb had
awakened him.

Outside, a few feet away, Belle Wilson spoke in a low
voice to the gunfighter Slocum had seen with Boots
Wyman.

He could have cut them both down where they stood,
but that wouldn't get any answers. Slocum doubted getting
the drop on the gunman and trying to take him prisoner to
question him would work, either. His mind raced, and he
came up with a plan that might produce a few answers.
Slocum went back into the room, downed the remnants of
the still-warm coffee, then hurried into the room where
Cara still struggled to hang onto life.

Slocum opened the window in the room and dropped out
behind the house. If he was quick enough about it, he could
fetch his horse and get back before the gunman finished his
business with Belle Wilson, whatever that might be.

7

Slocum had figured right. The gunman did not return to the fancy passenger car at the railroad siding, but went to the livery stables and took a horse. Whether he bought it or simply stole it, Slocum neither knew nor cared. From the easy manner of the gunman in the saddle, it was probably his own horse and gear arranged for in advance.

Trailing him was easier than it had any right to be. The gunman rode straight out of Bisbee, heading east into the mountainous Mule mining region there. Slocum had wondered if the man might not go south into Mexico, but there had not been a hint that he wanted to leave the country. Whatever he and Belle Wilson had argued about concerned the mountains ahead, not down Mexico way.

As dawn began crawling up the night sky and dragging itself piecemeal on to the horizon, Slocum fell back and let the rider continue at a slightly faster pace. When the man got near his destination, there might be sentries posted. Slocum wanted plenty of time to avoid them so he could finally find out what was going on. Wyman and his partners probably had had nothing to do with Lily's death, but Slocum's curiosity called for him to find out what had provoked all the furor in Bisbee. The way Cara had run straight to another of Wyman's sidekicks told Slocum he had blundered into something that had to be squared away

62

before he got down to serious hunting for the actress's killer.

Not much made sense to him, and that was as vexing as anything else that had occurred since leaving Tombstone. Cara had made love to him as a way of killing him. An old enemy had come into Bisbee riding in a fancy train car and acting as if he owned the town. Dumont had caught a bullet, killing him, and Cara was perched on the edge of a grave. But how did Belle Wilson and Wyman tie together?

Slocum's head hurt from too much thinking. Instead, he settled down and studied the desert landscape slowly flowing past, noting how they were gradually climbing into a mountain pass. From this well-traveled road dozens of smaller, rocky paths branched off leading to the copper and gold mines scattered throughout the area. Tombstone and Bisbee were both booming, producing enough high-grade ore to bring miners and prospectors flocking in. Spotted along the hillsides were dozens of shafts where men had clawed their way into the rock in search of gold, leaving behind tailings like that around a gopher hole. Slocum wished them all luck, that they all might find the mother lode they sought. He had tried hard-rock mining, and it was too exhausting for him. Chances of hitting it rich were far less than getting by simply earning a decent wage punching cattle, or even bucking the tiger in a game of faro and walking away with a few dollars.

Most miners wouldn't find more than enough color to keep themselves alive. The luckiest of those would stay alive long enough to see their dreams of wealth crushed like ore ready for smelting, then reduced to nothing but slag. They might find new professions where they could live out their days, but they would never be rich. But a few would, and those Slocum silently saluted.

The rider ahead of him on the road began stopping more and more frequently as if hunting for something. Slocum wondered if he knew exactly where he was headed or if he had to find landmarks and go by them. From what Slocum could tell, the man didn't have a map. That had made

Slocum think the gunman knew his destination only through oral description. At midday, the man found himself a shady area near a watering hole and pitched his gear down, flopping on top of it for a siesta.

Slocum considered what he might do. If he bulled his way into the camp, he could capture the gunslinger without a fight. But getting information from him might be a chore. Beyond that, the man had come to this godforsaken spot for a reason. Meeting someone, probably his boss, was the sole reason Slocum could see. Finding out what this owl-hoot and Belle Wilson had argued over might be interesting, but Slocum reckoned he could always get that from Belle later.

During the war Slocum had been the most patient of snipers, sitting on a hillside and waiting all day, if necessary, for the single flash of sunlight on a Federal officer's gold braid. A slow squeeze of the trigger of his Brown Bess, a single shot, and the enemy lacked a leader. He had done this more than once to the benefit of the Confederacy, but now all he did was sit in the hot sun and wait. No constant looking for a good target, no hint that he might be caught, nothing but tedium.

Slocum knew he might be lulled into thinking there was no danger if he simply sat and watched the gunman as he slept. Finding a sheltered place where a large boulder cast enough shade for his horse, Slocum put hobbles on the mare and then went off on foot, exploring the entire area.

It took him the better part of a hot, dusty afternoon to find all the approaches to the gunman's camp, making Slocum wonder why the man had chosen this particular spot. He was bottled up, with no way out of a box canyon if he chose to run in that direction. But then Slocum's quarry hadn't chosen this spot. Someone else had.

Belle Wilson? Something about that made no sense. Belle had argued with the man, and any business could have been taken care of while they thought Slocum slept inside the house. The gunslick had come out here on somebody else's orders.

Slocum drank deeply from his canteen, wishing he were in the other man's camp by the watering hole. He was getting mighty thirsty, and he knew his horse was similarly afflicted. There was no cure for the problem, however, until he saw who the other man was meeting.

Sunset lit the sky with brilliant reds and curious grays as if streaked by paint-dripped fingers, and finally Slocum heard the steady clop-clop of an approaching horse. To his surprise, the rider came not from Bisbee, but from deeper in the mountains. Trails ran parallel to the foothills, and the rider came from the south.

Slocum could not see the newcomer's face due to the gathering dusk, but knew instantly whom the other gunman met when he saw the limp. Boots Wyman joined his partner. Without wasting any time, Slocum slipped through the tumble of boulders and crouched behind a head-high clump of prickly pears not ten feet from the two men. He couldn't see them, but heard well enough to satisfy his curiosity about what was going on.

"What the hell do you mean you don't know where he went?" demanded Wyman. "I did some asking around town and was told he'd gone to that Wilson gal's house."

"Well, he wasn't there when I asked after him," the gunman said, his voice nasal and whining. "She said he wasn't there, and why'd she lie?"

"You shoulda looked. The other woman was there, wasn't she?"

"The one that tried to kill him? Sure, she was there. With a bullet in her gut, where else would she be? The sawbones is outta town and nobody knows when he'll be back. That was the only place she coulda been took, considering."

"He was there. I know it. You let him slip through your fingers."

"Why'd she lie? She's only a midwife and you know what he is. She flat out tole me he wasn't there," said the gunman.

"She might want the money on his head."

"A thousand dollars is a powerful reward for some drifter."

"Some drifter," scoffed Wyman. "He's more 'n that, and you know it."

Slocum missed the next few minutes of discussion as the two gunfighters huddled closer together and mumbled to themselves. He edged around the clump of cactus to get closer. Although wary of being seen, he wasn't as cautious when it came to brushing against the sharp spines of the prickly pear pads. He drove a long spine deep into his arm. Before he could restrain himself, he let out a yelp of pain.

Slocum froze, listening hard for any hint that Wyman and his partner had heard. Crouching lower, Slocum turned his attention to the long cactus spike in his arm. Grasping it firmly, he pulled slowly and steadily until it popped free of his skin. The relief of removing it was quickly replaced by new pain, burning pain caused by the dirt that had been left in the wound.

Then the cactus was the last thing on his mind.

"Don't," Wyman said, his six-gun leveled at Slocum's head. "Here I was raggin' on Prentiss 'bout losin' you, and you was spyin' on us the whole time."

"See? That blond bitch wasn't lyin' after all," Prentiss said. "This owlhoot was out here hidin' so we couldn't find him."

"Hidin'? No," Wyman said slowly. "I don't think he's been hiding out here at all. He followed you from Bisbee, that's what he did." Wyman moved around and motioned with his six-shooter. "Get to yer feet."

Slocum did as he was told, his hands away from his sides.

"Son of a bitch," Wyman said, getting a good look at his face. "Slocum!"

"You know him?" asked Prentiss.

"Hell, yes, I know him. He's the back-shootin' son of a bitch that shot me in the leg."

"Still stealing fancy-ass boots off dead Mexican shoe-makers, Wyman?"

"What's he sayin'?" Prentiss moved around so he could keep Slocum in a cross fire if things turned ugly, but he looked to his boss for an answer. Slocum couldn't dodge left or right without running down the barrel of a six-gun. Going back toward the watering hole where the outlaws had camped meant climbing through the thicket of prickly pear cactuses. One spine had burned as if it had been dipped in acid. Even to save his life, Slocum wasn't going to dive into the clump of prickly pear cactuses—but it might come to doing something desperate like that if he wanted to keep on living. If he bolted and tried to run in the only direction open, they'd both shoot him in the back. He knew Wyman wouldn't mind, and he doubted Prentiss would, either.

"Keep yer mouth shut, Slocum."

"He's not the one, is he, Wyman? Go on. Tell me he's not the one."

"Shut up, Prentiss. I don't know what to do with such a fine little gift bein' dumped in my lap like this."

Slocum dug his heels into the hard ground, ready to draw. Better to die going for his six-shooter than to let a skunk like Wyman just kill him.

"You mean you didn't tell him how you got those boots of yours, Boots?" Slocum bore down on the sobriquet to get Wyman's goat. Make him mad, make an opportunity to get the hell away from these two killers.

It didn't work.

"I know why you're here, Slocum," Wyman said. The gunman moved a bit so he had a better shot at Slocum.

"Why's that?"

"You want the money, too. You're not gonna get it. Me and Prentiss, we're gonna get it. Never had you pegged for a bounty hunter, but then you'd steal pennies off a dead man's eyes."

"Like you steal boots," Slocum said, but the goad failed completely this time. He saw it in the outlaw's eyes. Slocum changed his tactics. "Who're you after? How much is the reward? I assume you intend to bring him in dead."

"Dead's the way he's wanted," Prentiss said, puffing out his chest. "No way a snake like him's gonna stay alive."

"Shut up," Wyman said. "You talk too much, Prentiss." Wyman moved a bit more and motioned with the barrel of his pistol for Slocum to drop his Colt. Reluctantly, Slocum did as he was ordered.

He felt naked without the familiar weight at his left hip. He had the hunch he'd feel even more vulnerable soon.

"You just gonna shoot him down, Boots?" Prentiss was getting blood fever. Slocum could see it in his eyes and the way he jerked around, his gun shaking just a tad. But it wasn't enough of a movement off target for Slocum to take advantage.

"I ought to, but I think there's a better way."

Slocum didn't like the sound of that.

"See, Slocum, I been livin' with this gimpy leg you gave me. Out here in the desert, ain't so bad, but down in the Hill Country where I was born, now there I feel a nasty twinge ever' time it's gonna rain. And whenever it gets all stiff on me, I think of you. How I think of you." Wyman's lips compressed to a thin line that turned into a sneer.

"What you gonna do, Boots? If you're gonna talk him to death, let me plug him."

"Shut up," Wyman said mechanically. His eyes narrowed into piglike slits and the sneer turned into a broad grin. "I got bigger things planned for you, Slocum."

"Like you do for the gent you're tracking down?" Slocum asked.

"He's no concern of yours. Fact is, nothing's gonna concern you no more."

Wyman gestured for Slocum to precede him to the campsite. The small fire had sputtered out, but Slocum knew that the gunman wasn't inviting him in for a cup of coffee.

"Cut some stakes, Prentiss. We're gonna show Slocum here some real hospitality, Texas style."

"But we ain't in Texas," Prentiss said.

"Shut up and do as you're told. And you, Slocum, why don't you start stripping off your clothes. All of them."

"Not satisfied with stealing only boots now?" Slocum

had goaded Wyman into taking a swing at him, but Wyman misjudged in the darkness. The outlaw intended to lay his gun barrel alongside Slocum's head, but missed by an inch. The impact across the top of his head still knocked Slocum to his knees and gave Prentiss time to swing around.

"I got him covered. Get the stakes. Long ones. Ones he can't pull out of the ground," snarled Wyman.

Slocum was groggy and barely aware of Wyman and Prentiss ripping his clothes from his body, leaving him stark naked. But he was only too aware of how Wyman stretched him out spread-eagle on the ground, wrists and ankles secured with rawhide strips to the stakes Prentiss had driven deep into the hard ground.

Admiring his handiwork, Wyman looked down at Slocum and laughed.

"Don't worry 'bout getting too cold tonight, Slocum, because you're gonna be mighty warm tomorrow. You oughta be cooked to perfection before the sun's down another day. Come on, Wyman. Let's get out of here. I need to get some sleep and the sound of a man bawling for mercy'd keep me awake."

Slocum knew the real reason Wyman wanted to go. He could fantasize what Slocum would cry out, how he would beg and plead to be let loose. But Slocum would bite off his own tongue before a single word escaped his lips. That lack of pleading for his life would sting Wyman's pride more than anything else Slocum could do.

But the laughter of the two outlaws as they rode off didn't make Slocum feel any better about lying naked on the cold desert ground. And when morning came, he would cook alive.

He struggled to pull out the stakes until he was exhausted and his wrists were wet with his own blood. In spite of the biting cold, Slocum fell asleep until the first rays of the sun poking up over the mountains woke him.

Then the real torture began.

8

Slocum kept his eyes clamped firmly shut because his face was in direct sunlight. Brutal light. Burning light that seared skin and eyes and robbed him of his will to live, and it was hardly ten o'clock.

He refused to die. He had a score to settle with Boots Wyman and his scurrilous partner, Prentiss. But he was having an increasingly hard time concentrating his hatred on them. The more he tried to picture the two owlhoots in his mind, the more the image became a mirage, distant and wavering as if seen through a heat haze. Slocum tossed his head from side to side, ignoring the pain as a rock cut into his cheek, trying to get the sweat out of his eyes.

Sometime just before midday, sweating was no longer a problem. All the moisture in his body had been burned out by the intense Arizona desert sun. His tongue was swollen to the size of a saddle horn, and every breath he took rasped his lungs like sandpaper. But he refused to die.

"I won't give up," he said through his chapped lips and even drier mouth. "I'll kill you."

"You won't get the chance," Wyman taunted. "You're nothing, Slocum. You got no chance to kill me 'cuz I've already killed you. Your problem is, you jist don't know it yet."

"No," Slocum said, shaking his head, watching the

brightness of the sun dance from one side to the other through his eyelids. "I'm not dead. I'll get free and cut you down where you stand, Wyman."

"Go on, try to get loose. Your hands are numb, ain't they? I tied the leather thongs real tight. When you started bleeding, the rawhide got wet. It's dryin' out in the sun now. When rawhide dries, it . . ."

"Tightens," Slocum grated out. "I can feel it. Wrists and ankles. It doesn't matter if I cut off my hands and feet. I'm going to get you if I have to hobble to San Antonio and rip out your throat with my teeth."

"Don't argue with him, John darling," came Lily's familiar voice. "Relax, take it easy, let go and fly. Be free! You can join me then."

"No," Slocum shouted. His voice was hardly more than a whisper, but he fought. "I'm not going to die. You're dead, Lily. I want to find who killed you and make them pay. Somebody shot you from ambush. One shot. Damn good marksman."

"You carry on so, John. Don't. Give in. Come and be with me. It's so pleasant here."

"It's hell here," Slocum said. He blinked and opened his eyes. For the first time in hours, he wasn't staring into the burning disk of the sun. The respite came because the sun was passing behind a towering rock spire, but it would soon peek out on the other side and return him to searing agony.

Slocum looked around. He was alone. The fire pit with the remnants of a few mesquite branches furnished a bit of odor to his nostrils to convince him he was still alive. But where were Wyman and Lily? Craning his neck as much as he could in his weakened condition produced no result. His chin barely touched his chest, and when it did Slocum felt such knives of agony stabbing into his body that he almost passed out.

How easy it would be to give in as Lily had asked.

"Lily?" There was no answer. "Who killed you? If you're dead, you must know. You can see things from the other side. Tell me who shot you so I can kill them and join you."

Slocum thought this was a clever trick, but Lily never answered. He heard horses in the distance and knew Wyman and Prentiss had returned, but he didn't see them come to check their handiwork. His naked body screamed in pain from the sunburn, but it was his brain that kept him alive. If he died, he would never complete his mission.

He was a good soldier and always had been. Why had they assigned him to ride with Quantrill? Slocum relived the worst of the raids, the terrible times of finding that his brother had died, and that Bloody Bill Anderson hated his guts and gladly shot him when he complained about killing young boys in Lawrence, Kansas, and the long recuperation from the abdominal wound. So long. So very long before he got back to Slocum's Stand and found a carpetbagger judge had taken a fancy to it. Killing the judge and his hired gunman had been a civic duty, even if it had forced him to come West and dodge the wanted posters for judge-killing ever since.

But killing. He knew how to do that. He'd do that when he got free. Feeble tugs on his bounds produced no result, gave no hope. Slocum sagged to the ground and squinted again as the sun poked its fiery face out from behind the rock.

"They done you up good, didn't they?"

"I won't die, Lily. I won't do it."

"Lily?"

"I'll find Wyman and bury him with his boots on."

"The rawhide holding your right hand is cut. I'm leaving a knife on the ground. Free yourself or die. It will be an interesting experiment to see which it is."

"Don't go! Don't leave. Stay." Slocum realized he wasn't speaking and that his words were only guttural grunts. But he opened his eyes and saw a horse's tail flicking away black flies. Then the horse walked out of his field of vision.

Slocum sank back and worried over the last hallucination. He knew the others had been products of his tortured mind, but this one had seemed so real. His arm flopped across his eyes to shelter his face from the sun. It took some time before he realized that his right arm was free. His hand was no longer held down by the rawhide.

"Knife," he grated out, turning his head to the side. "Where's the knife?" He fumbled about for some time before his numbed hand banged into the sharp blade. It took the better part of five minutes for him to grip the knife and roll over to free his left hand. Two more clumsy slashes severed the ankle-binding rawhide near the stakes. He crawled away to get into shadows; then he passed out for a spell from the exertion.

When he came to, the sun was dipping low on the horizon and the desert was transforming itself into an icy wilderness again. The cold sent an invigorating thrill through Slocum's body, giving him the energy to sit up, use the knife on the knotted cords tied around his ankles, and roll onto his hands and knees. Simple movement caused him to shriek in agony.

He bit back the cry, knowing it would bring Wyman and Prentiss down on him in a flash if they heard. But he sensed only small animals around him, coming to the watering hole to refresh themselves before an evening of foraging. Along with them came the predators. Slocum clutched the knife as he rose to his knees and looked around. A wolf pack might try to kill him. A hungry coyote might consider him fair game. A mountain lion would be worse, smelling his raw flesh and blood and considering it an appetizer for the main course.

Slocum moved along a few feet, then had to stop. The pain almost caused him to black out. His entire front side had been sunburned. Not as badly as it might have been thanks to the mountains, the tall rock spire, and occasional clouds drifting through the otherwise empty Arizona sky, but enough to blister and burn. He reached the watering hole and plunged into it. The cold shock brought him out of his stupor enough to sputter and come to the surface of the shallow pond. Any other time he would have found the water tepid. Not now. It was like icy balm against his burns.

For some time Slocum lounged in the water until the feel of water began to irritate his burned skin. Slocum pulled himself to a comfortable spot and examined his injuries. While not as bad as they might have been, stretches of skin were increasingly showing blisters. Slocum hopped and hobbled to the prickly pear clump that had cut him off from meaningful escape earlier. He plucked the thick pads from the plant and went back to the watering hole.

Exhausted from this simple excursion, he recovered his strength, then fetched his clothing, the knife that he carried tucked away in his boot top, and most important, his trusty Colt Navy and gun belt. Using the knife, he peeled the cactus pads and extracted the thick juices from inside. Tentatively at first, then with increasing eagerness, he smeared the goo over his burned body.

The reaction of his skin as he applied the soothing natural salve was not as expected. At first it burned like the sun had returned to sear his flesh; then coolness spread until the pain faded like a bad nightmare. Slocum propped himself up and drifted into a light sleep. Often during the rest of the night he snapped out of the exhausted siesta, hand on his six-shooter when some faint sound brought him awake. The night was filled with danger, but Slocum was still in no condition to do much about it other than use his six-gun. If a mountain lion cub had come up, it would have bested him easily.

As morning dawned and Slocum came awake, he felt much stronger and even refreshed from his ordeal. A quick dip in the watering hole and a new application of prickly pear juices took the rest of the sting from his body. Only then did Slocum tentatively don his clothing. He found it best to drape the shirt over his shoulders without putting his arms through the sleeves, but he surprised himself by tolerating his jeans well enough. The only problem he had getting dressed was his swollen ankles. Putting on his boots proved a chore, but one he was up to.

Slocum shot an incautious rabbit and fixed it for his breakfast, using the lucifers from the tin in his shirt pocket to start a new fire. By the time he finished, it was midday and he found a spot in the shade to sleep some more. Only when the sun vanished beyond the western horizon did he stir, knowing he had unfinished business to tend to.

He drank his fill, wished Wyman and Prentiss hadn't stolen his horse and the rest of his gear, then applied more of the prickly pear salve before starting the long walk for Bisbee. The darkness was interrupted only by a sliver of moon, but it gave him enough light to find the road and start back. Several times during his hike Slocum wanted to simply give up and sit down, but fantasies of what he would do to Wyman and Prentiss when he caught them spurred him along.

And finding who had killed Lily. He owed the woman that much. Her murderer could not be allowed to go free.

As dawn again ignited the colors in the sky, Slocum slogged into Bisbee. The town was already stirring, readying itself for another day of commerce with miners and ranchers, but he had no idea where to go. Reporting Wyman and Prentiss to the sheriff would accomplish nothing, Slocum thought. Sheriff Yarrow had not shown himself to be that aggressive a lawman, and was as likely to dismiss Slocum's claims as nothing more than hallucinations from being afoot in the desert too long.

Slocum had no money. Wyman had searched his pockets and taken what little he had. His gear had been similarly stolen, along with his mare. That meant he wasn't likely to find much of a reception at a saloon where cash on the barrelhead was the inviolate rule. Hardly knowing it, he headed for the railroad depot, and then veered away when he saw the locomotive that had been on a siding was gone. Slocum didn't know if that meant Wyman had moved on or if the train had pulled out, leaving the gunman behind.

His feet gaining a mind of their own, Slocum soon found himself standing at Belle Wilson's front door. She had taken in Cara and nursed her. The murderous brunette was Slocum's only lead. If he could find why she had tried to kill him, he might get a lead on Lily's murderer—or discover what the woman's connection, if any, was with Wyman and his gang. From what he had heard, Slocum didn't think Wyman or Prentiss knew Belle, and considered her only another Bisbee resident beneath their contempt.

Slocum knocked and waited. He knocked again, and started to turn away as the door opened. Belle Wilson stood in the doorway, one hand clutching together the neck of a long robe. Her blue eyes widened as she studied him, going from toes to head.

"You look like you've been pulled through a knothole backwards," Belle said.

"Feel worse."

"You look like an Indian, all red-faced like that." She peered at him, then took a half step forward as she reached out. Her cool fingers brushed over his sunburned cheek. "You're running a fever."

"Got a whale of a burn."

"Cut up, too," she said, touching his right wrist and exposing the welt where the rawhide had cut into his flesh. "What can I do for you?"

Slocum started to answer, but his knees buckled. Belle caught him in surprisingly strong arms, turned, and lowered him to the floor.

"Come on in, why don't you, Mr. Slocum?" she said sardonically.

"Thank you, ma'am," Slocum said. He tried to sit up, but she pushed him back flat onto the rug where he had collapsed. He recoiled from the touch on his shoulder.

"You are a fright," she said, opening his shirt and studying him critically. To his surprise, Belle showed no revulsion at the condition of his chest. "Can you get over there onto the chair?"

"Got this far," Slocum said. He crawled halfway, then hoisted himself up using a table for support and collapsed onto the chair. Belle returned with a large jar of pungent-smelling ointment.

"I made this up special this morning, just in case," she said. "Let me apply it. It'll burn like a prairie fire and then will feel just fine. Get that shirt off. And show me everywhere else you need to be medicated."

"Everywhere?" Slocum found this funny and began laughing. It turned hysterical and tears ran down his cheeks, burning with their salty tracks.

"What's so funny?"

"You might have bit off more than you thought," Slocum said. He cast aside his gun belt, kicked off his boots, and shucked off his shirt. He looked at Belle. She seemed fascinated but not repelled.

"Well?" she asked. "I can guess what else is sunburned. This didn't happen by accident, did it?"

"Nope," Slocum said, gingerly pulling down his jeans.

"My," was all Belle said before she started applying her sweet-smelling unguent. In other circumstances Slocum would have found this stimulating, especially when her long fingers rubbed in the ointment over his belly . . . and lower. She tended him gently, and then reared back to study the result of her ministrations.

"Feels better," Slocum said.

"You must tell me how this happened. I suspect it's something to report to the sheriff."

"No need to bother him," Slocum said.

"You're probably right," she admitted. "I wish Doc Benbow was back. Since he's been gone this long, he might be on a bender. Or he could have moved on. He's something of a drifter, even for a doctor."

"Maybe he's a snake-oil peddler," Slocum said. His voice sounded distant, even to his ears. Relaxation washed over him, and the redness of his burns faded as he watched. Not much, but enough to make him think he was on the road to healing, thanks to the ointment. His own crude application of the prickly pear juice had helped. Belle's ointment had healed.

"I always thought so," Belle said, as from a distance as she helped him stretch out on the floor. From even farther away, he heard her chuckle. "A naked man in my front room. Who'd have thought it?"

Slocum tried to speak, but the words became jumbled as he slipped off to a long, needful sleep. He was not certain how long he slept, but his growling belly woke him with the message of hunger. Slocum stretched, felt the tautness of his skin but no pain, and then looked down. His skin was still reddish, but not unduly so. Where he had blistered proved worse. The skin was peeling and tender, but bearable. Even when he touched his privates there was no pain.

He looked at his hand and discovered it was coated with the thick paste Belle had smeared on him. Carefully reapplying it, he wondered how she had come to have so much ready when he needed it most. She had said she'd whupped up the batch that morning. Then his hunger grew and pushed thought of anything but food from his mind. All he had eaten in the past three days was one scrawny rabbit back at the watering hole.

Slocum rubbed his lips and realized how thirsty he was, too.

"Belle?" He called out the woman's name again, but heard nothing in the house. Getting to his feet, he wobbled about, got his balance, and then went to the woman's pantry, where he found some stale bread. He wolfed it down, drank some water from a pitcher, then raided Belle's larder for more food. She had a bit of cheese and a piece of beef that hadn't begun to turn moldy yet. Even if it had, Slocum would have eaten it. He was hungry enough to rip off the wallpaper and eat it, glue and all. A bit of old bread and meat was a banquet to him.

When his hunger was sated, Slocum sat in a chair and wondered where the blonde had gotten off to. He found the jar of ointment and applied more of it. While it cooled and cured him even more, he missed Belle's knowing application, the way her fingers had lingered as she applied the salve on certain parts of his anatomy, the constant soothing flow of words letting him know he was going to be better.

Slocum had to get better. He had to find Lily's killer—and get his revenge on Wyman and Prentiss.

Finished slathering himself with the unguent, Slocum stretched his tight skin again and felt the muscles responding properly. He was on the road to recovery. Carefully donning his clothing, he felt almost human again. He looked around, then frowned. Slocum crossed the room in three quick strides and opened the bedroom door. A quick look inside confirmed what he had suspected. Cara was gone.

"Where is she?" Slocum had heard the front door open and, without turning, knew Belle had returned. This puzzled him a moment; then he realized it was because of the hint of perfume she wore. He had smelled it before but couldn't place where.

"The woman you brought in a few days ago?"

"Cara," Slocum said. "Her name was Cara."

"I believe she mentioned that," Belle said. "Good, I see you found the food."

"You didn't have much."

"I haven't been here too long," she said.

"Why not? I thought you lived here in Bisbee."

"Oh, I come and go," Belle said vaguely.

"Like Cara? What happened to her? She didn't die." Slocum turned and faced the blonde and saw the emotions racing across her face. Once she realized he was studying her, a poker face replaced the panorama of her innermost thoughts.

"No, she didn't die. In fact, she said she was going home."

"Where might that be?" Slocum saw that Belle was going to lie. "Could it be that she returned to Yuma?"

This hit home with the woman. She tried to cover her shock at this, then gave in to the inevitable.

"Why, yes, that's where she went. Yuma. How did you know?"

"Cara shared a great deal with me," Slocum said, fishing for a reaction. But by now Belle was steeled against giving herself away any more.

"Do tell," she said.

Slocum pulled up a chair at the kitchen table and sank down. His legs refused to support him anymore. He was still recuperating from his ordeal.

"I've tired you out," Belle said, relieved at changing the direction of his interrogation. "Why don't you lie down? On the floor if you like. Or in the bed?"

"Out here's fine," Slocum said, having trouble keeping his eyelids open. "I need to catch a few winks; then I'll be on my way."

"There's no hurry, Mr. Slocum," she said. "Stay as long as you like. I rather enjoy your company."

That was all Slocum remembered as his tortured body demanded its due. This time he dreamed of what he would do to Wyman when he caught him.

And Belle's perfume. He dreamed of the woman's perfume.

9

Slocum dozed and occasionally went to get water. But after a few hours of napping and drinking, he grew restless. He sat on Belle's chair and wondered where the woman had gotten off to. He thought she was going shopping. But she could grow a basket of parsnips in the time she had been gone.

His thoughts drifted aimlessly, but slowly focused on a few items. He doubted Wyman and Prentiss would stray too far. They were bounty hunters looking for someone and, as of a couple days earlier, had not found him. If they thought their quarry was in Bisbee, they would stay until they found him and claimed their reward. Slocum decided that, since they had tried to kill *him* and didn't know they had failed, they would be in town or close by. This set Slocum onto a different path.

Who had saved him? He'd thought he was hallucinating when someone had cut the single rawhide bond on his right hand and left the small knife behind. Slocum had not been in any condition to think clearly, and had left the knife at the watering hole. He wasn't sure what good it would do having it as tangible evidence, but he might find its owner. He owed someone a giant debt of gratitude. Like bad deeds, Slocum always repaid good deeds done to him.

He turned grimmer as he stood and went to the bedroom

door to stare at the empty bed. Cara had lain there and now was gone. For whatever reason, it didn't appear that Belle Wilson had slept in the bed. Slocum frowned. Where did she sleep? He had stumbled to her door and apparently gotten her out of bed. Slocum went into the small room and began hunting through dresser drawers. He found a few items of women's clothing, but couldn't see Belle wearing any of it. It was almost as if she were an interloping cuckoo, sneaking in and taking over some other bird's nest.

He started to leave, thinking he was violating the woman's privacy by searching through her bedroom like he was a sneak thief. This was certainly not a good thing to do since she had taken him in and nursed him. But something was wrong. Slocum turned back to the dresser and looked again at the clothing, picked it up, and sniffed deeply. His head spun as he recognized the scent.

Lily Montrechet.

"How?" he muttered. He shook himself and tried to convince himself he was mistaken. Similar clothing, same smell? He inhaled deeply again and knew he was not wrong. He might not have a bloodhound's nose, but he was a keen tracker when he put his mind to it. Holding up the frilly clothing, he judged its size, and knew Lily would have fit her ample torso into this perfectly. Belle was a thinner woman, taller and more muscular. He knew this from the feel of her hands moving over him, just as Lily's had.

Slocum sat at the kitchen table and tried to make sense of it. There wasn't any way Lily's clothing could have been here in Belle's house. No way at all.

He couldn't shake the feeling he was missing something that would explain what his senses told him was true and his logic denied.

Slocum heaved himself to his feet, carefully strapped on his cross-draw holster, and settled the heavy six-shooter on his hip. He practiced his draw a couple times, learning the feel of taut, sunburned skin and accepting it as normal for the time being. If he had to use the six-gun in a hurry, he didn't want unusual aches and pains distracting him.

When he was sure he knew every blister and sore spot, he slid the pistol into the holster and went to look for Wyman and Prentiss.

Slocum had lost track of time, and wasn't even sure what day it was. From the ruckus in the Bisbee saloons, it must be Saturday night. The miners had come to town to hoot and holler, get as stewed as hooty owls on their meager stash, then go to church tomorrow morning all hung over before returning to their claims for another week of backbreaking work squeezing tiny flakes of gold or huge hunks of copper from the hard Arizona rock.

Walking up and down the main street, Slocum looked around like his head was on a swivel, studying the horses tethered in front of the myriad saloons, looking for his mare or some trace of Wyman and Prentiss. Something drew him to a saloon in a tent pitched near the edge of town. He poked his head past the canvas flap and checked the patrons in the smoky interior. The place had an impermanent look, but the bar itself was solid oak, highly polished and probably worth more than the stock of trade whiskey lining shaky shelves at the rear. He had seen operations like this before. The gin-mill owner would load the bar into the back of a wagon, take down the tent, and be in the next town before sundown the next day, always looking for the boomtowns and new gold strikes where money flowed the fastest.

Slocum started to back out of the saloon when he heard a loud voice from the rear. Changing his mind, Slocum slipped in and kept his back to the canvas, a dubious protection at best but better than nothing.

"Come on over, fellas. I got me a wad of greenbacks and they're burnin' a hole in my pocket. Let me stand the lot of you to a drink. Two drinks! Barkeep! Whiskey fer my friends!"

Slocum wondered where Prentiss had gotten so much money. The man waved it around, clutched in his grimy fist. The bartender was only too glad to relieve him of a large portion of the scrip in exchange for a couple bottles of cheap whiskey and a dozen shot glasses.

Prentiss poured clumsily, slopping more on the bar than he got into the glasses. The barkeep started to protest, letting Slocum know who owned this establishment. Then the man clamped his mouth shut and went to sell warm beer to a pair of miners at the other end. If Prentiss came through with the rest of his poke, the barkeep would be more than happy to clean up after his careless pouring of the tarantula juice.

Slocum settled down in a chair so he could keep an eye on Prentiss while the man drunkenly licked up the whiskey he had spilled on the bar. The man was so far in his cups that Slocum reckoned Wyman would come by sooner or later to fetch his partner. Then he would act. Until then, he enjoyed the show Prentiss was putting on.

"Sing!" The gunman threw his empty shot glass at the piano player at the rear of the tent. The man instinctively ducked and launched into a bawdy song, hardly taking notice of Prentiss. This was all in a night's work for the musician.

Slocum decided the piano player wasn't too bad a singer, but he kept his eyes fixed on Prentiss. The man insisted that everyone near him drink up. He didn't get any complaints from the miners. They had come to Bisbee to let off steam, and being given free drinks was like dying and going to heaven.

"Whatcha want, mister?" asked a tired-looking bar girl. Slocum gave her a quick once-over and dismissed her. The pretty waiter girls in San Francisco were better at their jobs of selling both liquor and themselves.

"Nothing to drink," he said. "I'm here to watch the show." He stared at Prentiss, but the gunman was too involved in doing a staggering dance to the music blaring from the piano.

"Got to buy something or you gotta go," the woman said. "Them's the rules."

"Then get me one of the free drinks he's passing out," Slocum said.

The waitress started to complain, then saw the steely

look in his eyes and backed off. She shrugged, went to the bar, grabbed a bottle Prentiss had bought, and returned to Slocum's table.

"Here," she said. "You want a glass, too?" She made it sound as if this was a great offer on her part. "Maybe something else, too? Like some company when I get off work, mister?"

"No."

"No?" She frowned. "You don't want a glass or you don't want me?"

Slocum fixed her with a quick look, took a long drink from the bottle, then put it down on the table with a loud click. She looked confused, then hurried off to tend to a knot of miners looking both thirsty and only half-drunk. There was a chance they'd become entirely drunk and maybe take her up on her offers of carnal sin.

More likely, she would get them staggering drunk and rob them. Slocum didn't care. He watched Prentiss and the show the gunfighter put on.

Slocum settled down so he could get to his Colt when the need arose. And it would. Prentiss was too drunk to take notice of everyone around him, but Slocum would come to his attention eventually. When it happened, Slocum wanted to remove Prentiss fast—but only if he could get Wyman, too. Boots Wyman was the one who had thought up the torture, and Slocum wanted to pay him back for it.

"Gettin' damn hot in here," shouted Prentiss. "Got to air out the place." He fired a few times through the canvas roof above, then laughed hysterically. "That ain't workin' so good. Got to take things into my own hands, I see."

Slocum sat a little straighter, thinking Prentiss was going to start spraying lead around. Instead, the gunman began stripping off his clothing. The piano player slowed, then picked up the tempo again when the barkeep shouted at him. But the entire tent saloon was becoming as quiet as a graveyard. All eyes were on Prentiss as he finished stripping off his clothes, save for his boots and the gun belt strapped around his bulging waist.

"Keep playin' them perky songs. I like 'em fast and I like 'em purty. Same as I like my wimmen!"

Prentiss flopped belly-down on the bar, then got to his feet and began his drunken dance. The sight of a man naked save for boots and six-shooter was enough to bring guffaws from the miners. They started clapping their hands and egging Prentiss on to even faster dance steps.

"Get down, you fool," shouted the barkeep. "You're scratchin' up my bar with them spurs."

Prentiss whirled around and pointed his six-gun at the saloon owner.

Slocum saw the gunman's finger tighten on the trigger and knew he would murder the barkeep where he stood.

Through the silence that had fallen, Slocum called out, "Don't do it, Prentiss. Shoot him and I'll kill you." Slocum stood, kicked back the chair, and squared himself, ready to throw down on the naked gunman. "Fact is, I'll kill you no matter what. First, though, you've got to tell me where Wyman got off to."

Prentiss stumbled, turned, and squinted hard to see who was calling him out.

"Slocum!" The name escaped his lips in a rush. "We kilt you. You oughta be coyote food by now."

"I was too tough for them," Slocum said. "Where's Wyman? I need to settle accounts with him, too."

"You son of a bitch!" Prentiss lifted his six-shooter and wobbled around, but being drunk didn't stop him from being dangerous. If anything, the whiskey might improve his aim.

Slocum cleared leather, aimed, and fanned off three rounds. For a heart-stopping moment, no one moved or spoke in the tent. It was as if time had halted its inexorable advance. Then Prentiss looked down stupidly at his bare chest and fell forward off the bar, crashing into the sawdust on the ground.

"Damn, mister," said the barkeep, kneeling by Prentiss and rolling the gunman onto his back. "You shot him three times."

"You kin cover the three holes with a silver dollar.

Never seen such shootin' in all my born days," said a miner with more than a touch of awe in his voice. "Lemme buy you a drink, mister. This one was a bad customer. You musta worked up a thirst cuttin' him down like you done."

"Thanks," Slocum said, slipping his Colt Navy back into its holster. "Any of you see this snake's partner?" He looked around the tent and saw a sea of shaggy heads shaking back and forth. Even if they had seen Wyman, they wouldn't know he was with Prentiss. "Where'd he get the money?" Slocum fumbled the wad of greenbacks out of Prentiss's discarded shirt and held it up.

Again the head-shaking and looks of growing concern. Slocum was asking questions like a lawman.

"Here, he wanted you all to enjoy yourselves. Drink until it's all gone," Slocum said, throwing Prentiss's money onto the bar. A loud whoop of glee went up. Slocum could have used the money, but wasn't going to take any of it off a man he had just killed.

Still, he wondered where Prentiss had gotten such a roll of money. When he and Wyman had caught Slocum out at the watering hole, they had been grousing about not having any money and needing to collect the bounty on the head of the man they were tracking.

"Tell me, old-timer," Slocum said to a short, balding man beside him at the bar. "Anybody else been killed in Bisbee lately?"

"Shucks, always somebody gettin' hisself kilt," the miner said. "Ain't heard of nobody else tonight. Might have been someone earlier in the week, though. I jist got into town an hour back."

Slocum sampled the whiskey and reeled from its potent kick. He had drunk too much without enough food in his belly.

He sank down into a chair and let the men work their way through a dozen bottles of the potent trade whiskey while he watched and waited. Some men had left the free booze and had gone outside. Word of the killing would spread, and if it got to Wyman soon enough, Slocum knew there would be a second body on the ground. For all he cared, they could bury both Wyman and Prentiss in the same grave and save the time, effort, and expense of digging two graves. But he wanted to be alert when the killer came, because Wyman would come with gun blazing, and Slocum wanted a clear head and quick hand.

Slocum whiled away the time waiting for Wyman to show up by coming up with new and inventive tortures for him. But he knew none of those would ever happen. He would be happy enough to see Wyman drop to the ground with the other three bullets from the Colt Navy's cylinder in his black heart.

At that thought, Slocum slid his pistol from the holster and set about reloading. He didn't want to face any killer with only half the number of rounds his Colt could hold. One shot would do, but it was prudent to make certain there were five backups. Then he took the derringer from his pocket—the pistol Cara had tried to use on him—and loaded it, also. He wanted this to end tonight.

Even as that thought crossed Slocum's mind, he knew it would not stop here. Finding Lily's killer remained a chore. How he was going to track down someone he hadn't seen and couldn't find any trace of in the desert was something beyond the possible. Slocum knew he'd just have to work that much harder to bring the murderer to justice.

"You do that?"

Slocum shifted his weight slightly in the chair. The sheriff had come into the tent saloon through a rent in the side wall. His two deputies made a grand entrance through the main flap, scatterguns ready to blow apart anyone foolish enough to oppose them.

"Evening, Sheriff Yarrow," Slocum said. "I settled a score with him."

"So you admit to murderin' the son of a bitch?" Sheriff Yarrow thrust out his chin truculently and hooked his thumbs in his suspenders. He could never get to his holstered six-shooter fast enough to stop Slocum since the lawman foolishly relied on his two deputies to shoot, if the need arose.

Slocum quickly estimated his chances of killing the sheriff, then gunning down the two deputies. They looked mighty good. He kept Cara's derringer hidden in his left hand while he placed his right on the table in front of him, just to keep the lawman calmed down a mite.

"He didn't murder nobody, Sheriff," called the saloon owner. "He stopped that owlhoot from damagin' my property and maybe killin' my patrons. You owe him a debt of gratitude, I say."

"Too bad he didn't kill yer damn piano player," Yarrow growled, making a sound deep in his throat like a stepped-on grizzly.

"He oughta get a gol-danged reward," piped up a customer. The rest of the miners agreed loudly. Slocum knew then that the money that had ridden so high in Prentiss's pocket had been well spent. If Yarrow tried to run him in for murder, he'd have a riot on his hands.

"You seen his partner?" Slocum asked. "Boots Wyman?"

"You keep your nose outta business that don't concern you," the sheriff said, trying to be stern about his warning. Slocum heard a tinge of fear in the lawman's voice. From the scorn Yarrow showed for Prentiss, Slocum doubted the sheriff much feared Wyman. But there was someone working with them that he did fear. Their boss?

"Who hired them? They were more than bounty hunters out for a few dollars reward. Who were they after? Who hired them, Sheriff?"

"Get that varmint's carcass outta here," Yarrow said cholerically, unhooking his thumbs and motioning to his deputies. They exchanged looks, as if saying they weren't paid enough to cart off dead bodies, then gave in to the inevitable. They slung their sawed-off shotguns on straps over their shoulders so they could each take a foot and began dragging the otherwise-naked Prentiss outside.

Slocum watched them go, no emotion at all in him now. He had evened the score with one of the men responsible for staking him out to die. Wyman wouldn't be far behind.

"You're playin' with fire if you keep after 'im," Yarrow said.

"Who's that, Sheriff?"

"Wyman, you damn fool. You better clear out or you'll have a dozen men worse 'n him on your neck."

"Then I'll have to reload a couple times to take care of matters," Slocum said.

"I'd think another man was drunk and braggin'. With you, I don't know if you might not be able to do what you think you kin do." Sheriff Yarrow spun and stalked out the main entryway. For a few seconds there was only silence; then the furor inside the tent broke loose, every man shouting at the man next to him about what had happened.

Slocum settled back down at the table to wait for Wyman. He doubted it would be long now.

10

Slocum caught sight of him before he came through the tent flap. Boots Wyman paced back and forth outside the tent saloon, as if wondering if he should enter. His flashy, hand-tooled boots gave him away, the sides catching light from inside and flashing every time he passed in front of the flapping canvas doorway.

Slocum leaped to his feet and drew his six-gun, ducked out the slit in the tent wall where Sheriff Yarrow had made his entrance earlier, then circled the saloon to come up on the gunman from behind.

Six-gun coming up, Slocum started to pull the trigger and end Wyman's worthless life. With the outlaw squarely in his sights, all he needed was determination and a few ounces of pressure. But resolve faded and the pressure on the trigger slackened when he centered the front sight on the back of Wyman's head. Too many questions had gone unanswered for him to take the man's life so easily.

"Move and I'll drop you," Slocum said. Wyman knew instantly how close he was to dying. His hands lifted from his sides, going out a ways to show he wasn't reaching for his six-gun.

"Slocum? That you? We got to talk."

"You did a powerful lot of that when you staked me out in the sun to die," Slocum said. His cold anger was fanned now, like slumbering coals in a campfire. He felt the heat rising in his face—and it wasn't entirely from the sunburn he had received because of Wyman's torture.

"You got it all wrong."

"Who hired you to kill me?"

"Nobody!" blurted Wyman. "I didn't even know you was in Bisbee till we came face-to-face out there east of town. We was after somebody else."

"Someone with a price on his head. Who?"

"You wouldn't know him. Name of Backus."

Slocum thought a moment of all the men named Backus he had ever known. There were a few, but none that would spark the interest Wyman and Prentiss had shown. The last time he had ridden a trail with anyone of that name, Jethro Backus had been killed in a stampede while they rode herd for a rancher down in Texas.

"Who hired you?"

Wyman let out a short laugh that was almost a bleat like a goat. His hands shook visibly now, alerting Slocum to the man making a play to either draw or run. Either way, Wyman was dead. Slocum's aim had not wavered a nickel's worth.

"I can't tell you. I promised. More 'n that, I'd end up dead. You don't know how treacherous the people are I'm dealin' with."

"Tell me."

"Put down that hogleg, Slocum!" The sharp command from behind him warned that the sheriff had returned. Worse, it gave Wyman the instant needed to jerk aside and then dive parallel to the ground.

Slocum fired, but the slug ripped through Wyman's hat, not his head. The gunman hit the ground hard and rolled into the saloon tent taking a shortcut under a flapping wall. Slocum fired a second time, ripping a hole in the canvas. Then his aim was spoiled by Sheriff Yarrow slamming his six-shooter down on Slocum's wrist. Pain shot all the way up to his shoulder, and he staggered slightly.

"No killin' in Cochise County," Yarrow snapped. "I

oughta run you in fer disturbin' the peace, if not outright at-
temptin' to murder a saloon patron."

Slocum was not above putting a slug in the sheriff's gut
and then going after Wyman, but he had lost sight of the
fleeing gunman. He knew he had to deal with the lawman
first before pursuing the man who wore boots stolen off a
dead man.

"He's Prentiss' partner," Slocum said, edging around
the irate lawman trying to see where Wyman had gone inside the saloon. The best he could tell, Wyman had run
straight for the rear and slid under the canvas wall like a
weasel avoiding a burlap-bag trap. By now he could be
halfway to Sonora. But Slocum doubted he would go far
because Wyman had given him the idea that the man he
hunted was still uncaught and unkilled.

"I don't care if he's the governor's no-account philan-
derin' son. You can't go round shootin' at him. If he broke
the law, he's mine."

"Then get him," Slocum said coldly. "He tried to kill me
and didn't come close." That was a bit of an exaggeration,
but he was wasting time and wanted to be on the gunman's
trail. "Why would Wyman be any different? You wouldn't
do anything about Lily Montrechet's death."

"There wasn't nuthin' to do 'bout that," Yarrow said, his
temper rising. "I got the peace to keep, not only in Bisbee
but in the rest of the county. There's process to serve
and—"

"And having nothing to do with killers like Boots
Wyman," Slocum said, keeping down his own anger. He
saw a flash of fear in the sheriff's eyes. "Who does he work
for? You know who he's hunting. Tell me."

"Why don't you just mosey on outta town, Slocum? We
don't need you pokin' your nose into matters that don't
concern you."

Slocum swung around, slid his six-gun into its holster,
and walked away from the sheriff, seething at the man's
cowardice. That was the only explanation Slocum could
come up with for the lawman not to go after Wyman. The

gunman was working for somebody powerful that the sheriff refused to cross.

Scouting around, Slocum finally spotted Prentiss's horse tethered down the street from the tent saloon. Knowing the man wasn't going to complain if he borrowed it, Slocum swung into the saddle. He needed to adjust the length of the stirrups for his longer legs, and the saddle itself was cheap and chafed in all the wrong places. He rode a few blocks, then decided part of the discomfort came from his sunburned body. This was the first time he had ridden since Wyman had staked him out to fry.

Slocum rode back to Belle's house and saw it was deserted. He dismounted and went inside, looking around. He felt as if he were breaking into a stranger's house and might be set upon at any instant. The jar of burn ointment she had whipped up still sat on the table where he had left it. With a quick swipe, he grabbed the jar and then looked around one last time.

The clothing in the dresser still bothered him. It was so much like Lily's choice in clothing. And the scent was hers. He had lain beside her enough to know. Slocum dropped the garments back into the drawer and closed it. Wherever this had come from was not the foremost question to answer. He had a mangy cayuse to track down before returning to the matter of Lily's killer.

Slocum tucked the burn unguent into the saddlebags and then mounted. He had to fight to stay astride the horse when a train whistle let out a long, loud screech.

"Whoa, boy, there, don't get excited." Slocum knew he had to learn the horse's foibles if he wanted to catch up with Wyman. The gunslinger had probably headed out of town to let things blow over, thinking Slocum would tire of hunting for him. Wyman was wrong. Slocum would go to the ends of the earth to settle accounts.

He rode slowly to the railroad depot and watched as a long white pillar of steam rose into the night sky as the train pulled away, heading north to join up with the main line. Slocum let the horse paw the ground and act as frightened as it wanted because it would eventually settle down once it realized there wasn't any danger.

"Come on, old fellow," Slocum said when the horse had finally calmed. He turned its head and walked the horse through the middle of Bisbele's red-light district, then to the adjoining street where the raucous saloons were spilling out their patrons into the street. Slocum avoided drunken copper miners intent on singing at the top of their lungs and lurching about to find a new audience in a new saloon, then reached the edge of town closest to the tent saloon where he had last seen Wyman.

The ground was as hard as stone and only a thin layer of dust covered it. The dust hardly kept a horseshoe print, and the slightest wind would erase the trail. But catching the ground just right against the bright moonlight showed Slocum tracks going straight out of town.

New tracks. Ones made within the last fifteen or twenty minutes. Eyeing the length of stride, Slocum realized that someone had galloped off. He would have bet a king's ransom that this was the direction Boots Wyman had taken, if he'd had even two dimes to rub together. As it was, he had to be content knowing he was on the man's trail.

Within a few minutes, Slocum was sure that he had the right set of hoofprints. The rider had gone to the main road leading eastward into the Mule Mountains, in the direction of the watering hole where Slocum had been staked out.

"Returning like a bad penny," Slocum muttered as he rode. He drew the rifle from its sheath and studied it in the moonlight, then thrust it back in disgust. It was about as he'd expected from a man like Prentiss. The rifle had not been oiled anytime this year, and trying to fire it might cause more damage to his hands and face than to his target. Slocum checked his Colt Navy as he rode, and knew it would do just fine when he finally ran Wyman to ground.

He rode faster, wanting to cut the distance between them. When he reached the campsite where he had been staked out, Slocum let out a snort of disgust. Wyman wasn't as much a creature of habit as he thought. No sign of the gunman meant he had not even paused to water his horse. Still, Slocum was sure he had followed the right trail. Although it was a possibility that Wyman had jumped the train going north, the gunman wasn't smart enough to leave Arizona Territory for good. He'd think he could avoid Slocum and finish his business, collect his bounty, and then ride off.

As he let his horse drink its fill at the watering hole, Slocum closed his eyes and tried to remember the lay of the land from the first time he had come this way. Mines dotted the hillsides, but this area had petered out already. He didn't recollect seeing any recent mining activity or even wagon tracks in the road showing that supplies were still being delivered to nearby miners. This was a lonely section of countryside, in spite of being on the main road heading for the bigger mines. Slocum reflected on how perfect this had been for Wyman and Prentiss to stake him out.

And how perfect it would be when he caught the man with the stolen boots.

He got back on the trail winding its way deeper into the mountains, and found ample fresh horse manure to tell him he was less than a half hour behind. Every sense alert, he surveyed the terrain ahead as well as the rims of the increasingly steep canyon walls. Anyone on the rim would never spot a rider below because of the inky, thick shadows along the canyon floor, but he could spot them outlined against the stars and illuminated by the silvery half-moon.

A horseshoe loudly striking a rock ahead warned Slocum he was close. He drew rein, dismounted, and advanced on foot, pistol in his hand. A slow smile crossed his lips when he saw Wyman on the trail just around a bend, studying his horse's right front leg. The gunman cursed a blue streak, then moved around out of sight and led the horse along. It was Slocum's turn to curse because Wyman put the bulk of the horse between him and a bullet.

Walking quickly, trying not to make a sound, Slocum moved to the far side of the road and then stopped. Wyman had vanished. Slocum canted his head to one side and heard the horse softly nickering. Turning in that direction, he found a narrow dirt path leading down a steep incline. He followed it and came to a well-established campsite.

Wyman had tethered his horse in a natural corral formed by boulders, and a rope hung across the narrow opening between them as he worked to light a fire. Slocum hung back a moment until the fire blazed brightly. Then he stepped out, six-gun pointed at.

"Hands up, Boots. This time the sheriff's not around to save your worthless hide," Slocum said.

Wyman's hand flashed for his six-shooter, but he fumbled, half-drew the gun, and then dropped it onto the ground. He started to reach for it, but Slocum cocked his six-shooter. The metallic click echoed through the still night like a death knell.

"You wouldn't shoot me in cold blood, now would you, Slocum?"

"In a heartbeat, you son of a bitch." Slocum felt every blistered spot, every reddened area of his body screaming at him to end this once and for all. But he held off. "Who're you working for?"

"I told you, I can't say."

"Then it'll be another secret carried to the grave."

"Wait! Wait, Slocum. If I tell you, will you let me go?"

"After what you did to me?"

"Look, we can dicker, can't we? You just turn me over to that hick sheriff back in Bisbee. He'd see justice done." Wyman was turning antsier by the second because he knew he had made a fatal mistake not killing Slocum outright when he had the chance. "Or you could take my boots. Yeah, that's it. Take my boots and make me walk wherever. I'd go to El Paso and you'd never see me again."

Slocum didn't bother telling Wyman that if he drilled him through the heart and left him for the buzzards, he'd never be bothered with seeing him again, either. But Slocum had too many questions, and Wyman was likely the only one who could answer any of them.

"Do you know who killed Lily Montrechet?"

"I . . ." Wyman swallowed hard, then shook his head. "I'll tell you what I know. I won't guess."

"You'll do as you're told," Slocum said tiring of the interrogation. "What about Cara? Dumont knew her."

"Her? Yeah, Dumont and her were . . . friends. More 'n that. He knew her over in Yuma. We ended up on opposite sides this time, but she worked for—"

"Go on. Tell me," Slocum said.

"She worked for Lady Death. Leastways, she used to."

Slocum stared at Wyman. The man was terrified to even mouth the name, and it told Slocum nothing.

"Who's that?"

"She's 'bout the worst killer this side of the Mississippi. Never fails. She's a crack shot."

"She killed Lily?"

"I don't know that, Slocum. But Cara would know. She worked for her, I think. She bragged on it to Dumont. She might have been lying to impress him. You know how them whores can be. But she mighta been tryin' to scare him off so she could keep the bounty money for herself."

"What's this Lady Death's name?"

"Don't know for certain," Wyman said. His eyes gleamed like a cat's in the guttering firelight. He saw he had information Slocum wanted that might save his good-for-nothing life. "But I think I know. Her and me, well, we're almost working for the same person, but on opposite sides of the fence."

"That doesn't make any sense."

"The money all comes from the same place, but them folks are all crazy, payin' to get people killed when there's no reason for it."

"Start giving me names. Who do you think killed Lily?"

"Lady Death, I told you. She was over in Yuma and I seen her with Cara. Not good, mind you, but enough to make me think she's—"

The rifle report echoed up and down the still canyon. For a moment Boots Wyman stood stock-still; then he reached for the tiny red spot blossoming on his chest. His fingers came away wet with his own blood. He looked up at Slocum and said in a husky whisper, "Lady Death."

Those were his last words. Wyman collapsed on the ground, falling into the fire he had started. His clothes caught fire, but Slocum didn't bother trying to put out the flames. He was already diving for cover and looking for Wyman's killer.

Lady Death.

11

Slocum was torn between hunting for the deadly sniper and going to Wyman to see if there was anything on the man's corpse that might tell him more of what he wanted to know. Deciding that Wyman wasn't going anywhere, Slocum slipped away into the dark, going away from where he thought the sniper had hidden, then made a wide circle. By the time he reached the area best suited for making the killing shot, Slocum realized he was all alone in the night.

After more than ten minutes scouring the area, he saw the glint of moonlight off spent brass. He picked up the shell and looked at it. If he had found anything worth mentioning, he couldn't tell what it was. The .45 shell fit about every rifle, and a whale of a lot of six-shooters resting on men's hips, in these parts. Slocum was certain the report had been that of a rifle. With the same precision that had stolen away Lily's vitality, the killer had robbed Wyman of his life, too.

"One shot, one kill," Slocum said, appreciating the expertise although he knew eventually that he would have to bring the shooter to bloody justice. He wondered if the sniper and the mysterious Lady Death that Boots Wyman had spoken of were one and the same. More than once Slocum had come across a woman with a remarkable facility for marksmanship, but they had been in sideshows and

100

made their living potshotting clay pipes and small glass targets filled with feathers. It took a special coldness in the heart to sight in on another human being and then pull the trigger.

Lady Death.

If Wyman hadn't been lying, Slocum was up against a deadly foe.

He circled the area hunting for tracks, but found none. A half hour later, he found where the killer's horse had been tethered to a mesquite tree. The horse had nibbled away some of the mesquite bean pods while waiting, keeping it quiet. But the identity of the rider who had mounted and trotted off toward Bisbee remained a mystery. The few footprints in the sand were indistinct, but lent some credence to the killer being a woman. The tracks were half the size of the amorphous imprints Slocum left when he walked on the sandy arroyo bottom, and not as deep. But this was pure speculation, and his interpretation might have been influenced unduly by Boots Wyman's frightened confession.

Turning back to the campsite, Slocum followed the stench of burning flesh and knew he might have taken a few minutes to put out Wyman's blazing clothes. He pulled his own bandanna up to cover his nose to rob the stench of some of its gut-turning power, then went to the outlaw. Slocum knelt and rolled the man's charred body out of the fire pit.

Wyman's body had snuffed out the fire, and his clothing had burned for only a couple minutes. Using the muzzle of his six-gun, Slocum poked through the remains of the man's pockets. A small chunk of cardboard fell to the ground. Slocum lifted it and stared at it. While there wasn't much left, it was about the right size to be the corner of a train ticket. Since Wyman, Dumont, and Prentiss had come into Bisbee on the train from El Paso, this meant nothing.

But a closer examination showed the last two letters on the destination.

MA.

"Yuma?" Slocum wondered aloud. Had Wyman held a ticket to Yuma? Or had he come from there and had lied about El Paso? Slocum slid the piece of ticket into his shirt pocket, then continued searching. Prentiss had flashed a wad of greenbacks, but all Wyman had on him were a few small coins and a gold double eagle. Stealing money off a dead man wasn't something Slocum cottoned to much, but he had done worse in his day. Besides, this barely compensated for the loss of his horse and gear. He had lost his spare Colt Navy in his saddlebags and his other change of clothes. Twenty-two dollars and a few cents didn't cover all that, not by a country mile.

Slocum stood and stared at the dead man. He stripped off Wyman's gun belt and tugged off the boots the man had been so proud of having stolen. Then Slocum set about digging a shallow grave he could cover with rocks to keep the coyotes away, for a while. He then went to Wyman's horse and searched the saddlebags.

A smile came to his lips. Wyman had gotten rid of most of Slocum's possessions, but had kept the spare Colt Navy. Slocum tucked it into his belt, tied Wyman's flashy hand-tooled boots together and draped them over the saddle, then led the horse back to where he had left his own horse—the one he had taken from Prentiss.

Slocum rode back to town, keeping an eye peeled for any ambush along the trail. He doubted the sniper would resort to such a tactic, though. Whoever had killed Wyman could have plugged Slocum in the back with the first shot, then taken out the gunman without much more effort. And if the sniper was the same one who had killed Lily, then Slocum had escaped death twice.

More than worrying about a bullet, he hunted for any trace of a rider to give him some clue to the shooter's identity. The road stretched lonely and long all the way into Bisbee. As he rode down the main street, he saw that most of the miners had finished their drunken binges and either were passed out on the boardwalks of town or had made their way back toward their claims. Some might remain in town for church services, but Slocum wasn't interested in them as much as he was the sheriff and his whereabouts.

He dismounted in front of the town jail, took down Wyman's gun belt and pistol, and went to the door. He rapped twice, but there was no answer from inside the jail-house. Slocum tried the door, but it was locked. He hung Wyman's gun on the latch, decided the man's horse, with the boots strung across the saddle, was just fine tied to the hitching post in front of the sheriff's office, then mounted and rode off.

As he rode, Slocum saw life coming into businesses other than the saloons. Dawn was still a half hour off, but the activity was boisterous and widespread, causing Slocum to rein in and call to a man busily sweeping off the porch in front of his bakery.

"What's the big stir?"

"You musta jist come to town, mister," the aproned man said, not looking up from his diligent sweeping. "He's comin' to town again. Biggest thing in a spell for Bisbee."

"Who's that?" Slocum saw four men unrolling a long canvas banner and struggling to string it across the main street. It spelled out WELCOME. Others prepared as if the President himself was coming to town, but for the life of him, Slocum couldn't believe President Garfield would come out West, especially to Bisbee. But the preparations going on with increasing industry showed somebody important was coming.

"He's the biggest thing to come to Bisbee since the Copper Queen Mine opened," the man said, finishing his cleaning. He leaned on the handle of his broom and looked at Slocum for the first time. "You still cain't figger it out? I'm talking about Norbert Peake, that's who."

Slocum felt the memory of the name lightly brushing around his brain, but like a spiderweb, it vanished as he reached out to touch it.

"The owner of the Arizona Central Railroad. That's who I'm talkin' 'bout."

Slocum shrugged. A railroad magnate meant nothing to

him, but obviously anyone putting a spur line into town made it easy to get the copper, silver, and gold ore moved to smelters.

"Thanks," Slocum said, but before he could ride on he heard someone shouting his name at the top of his lungs. Slocum turned in the saddle, his hand going to the ebony handle of his six-shooter. He relaxed when he saw Sheriff Yarrow hurrying toward him.

"Git yerself off that horse, Slocum."

Slocum knew the sheriff had been to his jailhouse and found Wyman's gun belt and his horse with the fancy boots draped over the saddle.

"You all excited about Norbert Peake coming to town, too, Sheriff?" Slocum asked.

"I don't want you runnin' round town, causin' trouble. Not when he's here," Yarrow said. "I gotta keep the peace, and the whole of Cochise County's more 'n I can handle."

"You've got deputies," Slocum pointed out. "What trouble are you looking for when Peake gets here?"

"What did you have in mind?" shot back Yarrow. "I wanna make sure you don't go causin' any uproar like you been doin'."

Slocum knew then that the sheriff hadn't been to his jail and found Wyman's effects. He would have been more specific about what he thought of as trouble.

"I'm moving on, Sheriff. Some of my business is finished. Think I might head on over to Yuma."

"Why Yuma?" The sheriff sounded suspicious.

Slocum wasn't inclined to tell the lawman his reasons.

"It's not Bisbee," he said simply.

"When you goin'?" Yarrow looked up at him suspiciously. "You leavin' 'fore Mr. Peake gets into town?"

"Can't say. When's he arriving?"

"Noon."

"I'll be long gone by then, Sheriff."

Yarrow studied him closely, thumbs locked into his suspenders; then he suddenly nodded and made a dismissive motion with his hand, as if shooing away flies. Slocum snapped the reins and got his horse moving along at a steady walk, leaving the lawman behind in the middle of the street. There was no reason to deal with a peace officer who wouldn't investigate the murder of a woman in his jurisdiction. As he rode, Slocum felt better by the minute because he wanted to find Lily's killer himself. Jail or even hanging wasn't good enough.

"Lady Death?" He wondered if Wyman had been dealing from the bottom of the deck and telling him whatever had come into his head. If the tale was wild enough, Wyman might have prolonged his own life. Then Slocum wondered if there might not be a sliver of truth to what Wyman said. Somebody had killed him, somebody who was a damned good marksman.

As good as whoever had killed Lily.

Slocum found himself riding toward the rail yard for no good reason other than to be contrary. He meant to go to Yuma, but taking the train was a quicker way of getting there to track down Cara than riding across the impossibly hot Sonora Desert this time of year. Hooking a leg around the saddle horn, he leaned forward to watch the preparations being made at the depot for the arriving railroad magnate. Slocum wasn't certain that even the President of the United States would get such a welcome.

"Why, I didn't expect to see you again."

Slocum jumped at the words. His mind had wandered along those steel tracks all the way to Yuma and what he had to do when he found Cara. She might not know who had murdered Lily, but Slocum wanted to find out why the woman had been so intent on plugging him. He had been suspicious of her from the first, but he had to admit she surely was good in bed. Turning, he looked down at Belle Wilson. The woman brushed back a strand of her blond hair when a hot gust of wind blew it down across her eyes. She wore the same dress she'd had when he had seen her last.

"I didn't expect to see you, either," Slocum said, touching the brim of his dusty hat in polite greeting.

"How's the sunburn?"

"The salve worked miracles," he said.

"I did enjoy applying it, too," Belle said, shyly averting her eyes as she spoke. This put Slocum on guard. There was nothing demure about this woman. When she looked back up, her blue eyes boring into his, the look was as bold as brass. "Why don't I apply some more? The jar's still on the table."

Slocum started to tell her he had taken it, then realized she had not returned to the house once she'd left. What her •business might have been to take her away so long, Slocum couldn't say, but it seemed like something he ought to find out.

"You getting ready to greet the railroad owner?" Slocum saw the flash of shock on Belle's face, but she covered quickly.

"You always surprise me, John," she said. "I was on my way back home. Come with me."

"And you'll slather that salve all over me again?"

She hesitated, then grinned wickedly. "Of course I will," she said. She licked her lips slowly, then turned and flounced off with a twitch in her git-along that would have drawn him even if he hadn't been interested in finding what she was up to.

Slocum dismounted outside the small house as Belle went to the door. She reached out and hesitated before opening the door. He saw her suck in her breath, then go inside quickly. Slocum wished he could see her face, but the cool dark interior hid any chance of watching her expression. He swung the reins around the hitching post and went in. For a second he'd considered taking the burn cream with him, but decided to see how Belle reacted when she couldn't find it.

He stepped into the house, closed the door behind him, and forgot all about catching the sultry blonde in any kind of gaffe. She stood in the doorway leading to the small bedroom, naked to the waist. Slocum smiled slowly, then began unbuckling his gun belt.

"Don't hurt yourself," she chided. "I know what all was sunburned. It must be getting mighty tight in those jeans 'bout now."

"Surely is hot," Slocum agreed, stripping off his shirt as he approached her. He drank in her beauty. He had known the blonde was lovely, but without the somewhat shabby blouse she turned gorgeous. Her unblemished milky white skin flowed from her neck, down her arms and chest, and up to the coral tips of her firm, high-placed breasts. She moved slightly, shifting her weight from foot to foot, causing those wondrous mounds of succulent flesh to sway beguilingly. As he stared at them, Slocum saw the nips harden with excited blood pumping hard into them. Belle was as excited as he was, no matter how she tried to maintain a cool, aloof attitude.

From those tempting jugs, that creamy flesh flowed down to a small wasp waist. Lower he could only guess, because she wore her skirt low on her hips, hiding the more intriguing regions.

Slocum stopped in front of her, reached around her waist, and pulled her close. He felt her tight, taut nipples crush into his chest. His skin was still warm from the sunburn and tender, but this only added to his arousal. He felt her breasts crush down as he bent and kissed her hard on the lips. For a moment, Belle fought the embrace; then she melted in his arms and returned the kiss with all the passion with which it had been delivered.

His hands roamed her bare back as they kissed. His fingers traced out the bones in her spine and moved lower, always lower, until his hand slipped under the waistband of her skirt. Her buttocks rippled under his fingers as he stroked over the fleshy curves. Using this handhold, he pulled her even closer. She parted her legs and wrapped her thighs around his upper thigh and began rubbing herself like a friendly feline.

Belle did everything but purr as Slocum began exploring even more of her willing, supple body.

Her arms wrapped around his waist, and she began slip-

ping down to her knees. As she went, her lips brushed
across his chest and belly, and her fingers duplicated the
efforts his made. Belle's long, slender fingers worked under the waistband of his jeans, and finally the buttons holding the front shut popped open. As they opened, one by
one, Belle's mouth was there to give encouragement every
time. Slocum felt her hot breath gusting across his groin.
By the time his manhood jumped out, long and tall and
proud, her lips closed on the purpled tip.

Her lips kissed him, licked and teased, and then the tip
of her flicking tongue began dragging itself wetly along
the sensitive underside of his steely stalk. Slocum sagged a
little in reaction. Belle followed him. When he straightened
his legs again, she managed to rid him of his pants like she
was shucking an ear of corn. He stepped free of his jeans
as she reared back and looked up at him, lust burning in her
blue, blue eyes.

"I want you, John," she said. "I can't explain why, but I
do."

"No need to explain what comes natural-like," Slocum
said. He couldn't get enough of her naked beauty. There
wasn't a mole or blemish anywhere he could see. Her nipples pulsed with need with every frenzied beat of her heart
and begged for his lips to suckle, to lick and kiss and gnaw.

"You don't understand," Belle said, leaning back, her
elbows braced on the floor.

"I'll make you understand why," Slocum said, dropping
to the floor and running his hands up beneath her skirt,
pushing the unneeded fabric back to expose her legs. He
kept his eyes on her face. Belle closed her eyes and
breathed more heavily now. Her breasts rose and fell delightfully as her passions mounted. She gasped, arched her
back, and spread her legs wide when his hands reached the
vee of her legs.

"There, oh, yes, there. I need you so now, John. Now!"

She reared up and grabbed at his upper arms, pulling
him forward. Slocum had expected to make love on the
bed, but neither of them wanted to take the time for that.

He leaned over, his mouth seeking hers. Their lips locked as he sank down, his weight pressing her into the hard floor.

Belle wiggled and writhed under him, trying to get herself into proper position. Her fingers slipped between their bodies and surged low, grabbing his manstalk and pulling it insistently toward the spot where his fingers had roved only a few seconds earlier.

Slocum ran his hands under her buttocks, cupping the firmly fleshed half-moons, then lifted. Belle obliged, rising off the floor to allow him to ease himself forward into her yearning cavity. Slocum's arrowhead-tipped shaft touched her trembling nether lips, paused a moment, then moved forward like a fleshy battering ram. She gasped at his slow, inch-by-inch entry into her innermost depths.

Slocum felt her tightness surrounding him, and relished the moistness, the heat, the sheer sensual pleasure of being within her. His hips levered forward as he lifted himself up on his hands and sank fully into her center. From this position he could look at her face. Never had he seen such a play of emotions as on Belle Wilson's face at this instant. There were the expressions he expected.

Pleasure. Anticipation. Wanton need.

But there was also a loathing, a hesitation, as if she participated in this lovemaking in spite of her own better instincts. Somehow, this spurred Slocum on to do his best. He wanted to erase her doubts for all time.

He withdrew slowly, a lewd sucking sound betraying the tightness of the tunnel he had been inside. When only the thick head of his manhood remained within the pink curtains of her nether lips, he paused, let her know he was toying with her, then slipped forward again. Slowly. Tormenting her with his flesh. Giving her reason to thrash about beneath his weight.

He found his deliberate movement was beginning to weigh heavily on him. She was tensing and releasing those powerful inner muscles to give him an erotic massage unlike anything he had ever felt before. If there had been hes-

itation on the blonde's part before, it was now gone. She
was giving as good as she got. Her body rose off the floor
to meet his every inward thrust, and then sank back as he
retreated.

But Slocum wasn't able to resist her feminine wiles. He
felt the pressures mounting within his loins that could not
be denied much longer. Belle was too much of a woman for
him to maintain this slow, deliberate pace. He thrust forward, faster this time, felt the arousing friction along his
length, and then remained within her. He rotated his hips,
grinding his crotch powerfully into hers. Their bodies
strove, one against the other, until both were bathed in
sweat and panted harshly from the sexual exertion.

Then Slocum pulled back, slid his hands under Belle's
curvaceous buttocks again, and drew her toward him. He
sank deeply into her as he lifted her rump from the floor.
Twisting and turning, they began to move with greater
speed, more power, more profound strokes. Belle began
crying out as her desires broke like waves against a distant
shore.

She thrashed about, but Slocum held her tightly. His
own need was mounting. Then it passed the point of no return. Repeatedly, he slammed hard, drove forward as if he
might tear her in two, sank balls deep within her moistly
yielding female sheath, until he exploded. He felt the heat
deep within him rising slowly, then building speed to erupt
potently.

Locked together, they soared on the erotic winds of
their shared sensation. Then Slocum drifted down and got
his knees under him so he could rock back and study the
woman again. Even with her skirt wadded up around her
trim waist, her legs spread lewdly and her breasts bare, she
was gorgeous.

Any trace of doubt Belle had shown before was now
gone.

Both started to speak at the same time, but were
drowned out by the loud, shrill shriek of a train whistle.
They laughed and disengaged their bodies, Belle sitting up

with her back against the bed. She pulled down her now-rumpled, wrinkled skirts.

"You continue to surprise me, John. Pleasantly so," Belle said.

"Should we go meet the train?" Slocum thought he had jabbed Belle with a knife. Her content, sated expression changed to one of suspicion.

"Why do you say that?"

"I've never seen a railroad president. If this Norbert Peake's taken the time to come here, there's no reason I shouldn't take the time to go see him."

"No!"

Slocum looked sharply at her. Belle was reaching for her blouse and hurriedly putting it on. He was sorry to see her fine breasts vanish beneath the ratty material, but her unexpected response was more disturbing.

"Why not?"

"We can spend the rest of the day here. Just you and me." Belle wasn't too convincing with her effort to keep him there, and she saw how her obvious come-on failed. She rushed on. "Let me get you a drink."

"I could use one. Making love to you worked up a powerful thirst," Slocum said. "Where's my other boot?"

"Over yonder," Belle said, pointing. "You get it on while I fix us a couple drinks."

Slocum watched as she went to the cabinets in the kitchen and hunted for two tumblers to hold the whiskey from the bottle she pulled out from one of the cabinets. Belle glanced over her shoulder, and Slocum hastily turned his attention to pulling on his boot. But he kept an eye on her as she reached into a small pocket in her skirt and then blocked what she did from him.

Slocum knew when anyone added a knockout drug to his drink, but he took it from her nevertheless.

"Drink up," she said. She clinked her glass with his and started to drink.

"What's that? Looks like some portly old man coming up the walk," Slocum said.

"What!" Belle's eyes went wide. She put her glass down on the table and rushed to the door to peer out. When her back was turned, Slocum switched his whiskey for hers. "There's nobody out there. You're seeing things, John."

He shrugged and said, "Guess I'm still a bit cross-eyed from such strenuous exercise."

"Drink up," she said, taking the glass from the table and downing a hefty slug of the potent liquor. Slocum downed his in one long draft, licked his lips, and set it down. Belle continued to work on hers until it was finished in a somewhat more ladylike fashion.

"What now?" Slocum asked.

"We can try out the bed this time."

"I'll see if I can keep up. You tuckered me out the first time."

"You're such a man, John, I know you'll be up for it." Belle laughed and went to the bedroom door, slowly taking off the blouse she had put on only a few minutes earlier. Slocum watched as she went to the bed and sat down. For a moment, blouse half off, Belle wobbled. Then she fell onto her side. The knockout drug had worked quickly.

"Why did you want me to stay here with you?" Slocum wondered aloud. He hiked her feet to the small bed, then chastely closed her blouse. Asleep—passed out—Belle Wilson looked so peaceful, Slocum could hardly think any ill of her.

But she had tried to drug him. He settled his gun at his hip, then left her to find some answers to the dozens of questions boiling up inside him.

12

Slocum started to mount his horse, but heard the cheers coming from the railroad depot down the road a ways. He knew Belle was going to be out like a light for some time, so he left his horse where it was tethered and sauntered to the edge of the crowd gathered along the railroad tracks. In the distance sounded another long, shrill whistle blast.

"That the president of the Arizona Central Railroad?" Slocum asked a woman straining to see over the heads of those in front of her.

"Who else? Mr. Peake's responsible for the success of this town. Bisbee would be just another boomtown if he hadn't built this spur from the main line. He's a hero!"

Slocum saw that the train had stopped so the engineer could creep forward slowly and make a grand entrance for the citizens of Bisbee. The way the people acted, this was a real treat. The train inched closer, and the roar from the crowd grew in volume until Slocum had to turn away. He wasn't much for big congregations of people. Looking around, he saw a siding with a couple of passenger cars waiting to be hooked onto the engine for a trip back to the main line and then west to Yuma. Slocum circled the crowd to the outside of the depot and rapped on the glass window to get the ticket agent's attention.

113

"What is it?" the man asked irritably. "Can't you see? Norbert Peake's come to town!"

"I want to leave town. How much for the ticket to Yuma for me and my horse?"

"Four dollars," the ticket agent said automatically, still distracted by the approaching train with the fancy parlor car with the owner of his railroad in it.

"When's the train leaving?"

"What? Oh, whenever Mr. Peake frees up his engine. He's gonna stay in Bisbee for a few days, him and his missus."

"He brought his wife along?" For some reason, this surprised Slocum.

"Yes, sir, shows how much he thinks of us here. She's a real classy lady, Mrs. Peake is."

"An hour? Two?"

"Oh, the schedule," grumbled the ticket agent. "Call it an hour to get the engine turned and the cars hooked on. Got a couple more freight cars to swing in, too. Some ore, but not much this time since we got two passenger cars."

"That many people leaving Bisbee?" Slocum's question fell on deaf ears. The ticket agent had already passed across the cardboard stub and returned to peering out the window onto the platform. Slocum fingered the ticket, then fished in his pocket for the one taken from Wyman after he'd been killed. The color was the same, but all the cardboard stock was likely to be identical for any particular railroad company, especially out in a jerkwater town like Bisbee.

Slocum shrugged it off and went back to the edge of the crowd to see a large-bellied man emerge from the rear door and stand on the back platform of his parlor car. He was dressed in a cutaway coat and had a fancy wine-colored cravat with a headlight diamond gleaming in the morning light. The man doffed a tall black silk top hat and bowed slightly in the crowd's direction.

The cheer that went up hurt Slocum's ears. He would have left to find a quieter spot to wait for the trip to Yuma and Cara, but he was drawn by the railroad magnate's sheer presence. Norbert Peake acted as if he'd known he would receive such adulation from the people of Bisbee. It was his due and he exuded that overweening confidence from every pore.

"Ladies and gentleman!" Peake called in a bass voice that rumbled up from deep in his chest and rolled out like thunder. "Thank you for this fine welcome!" He waited several seconds for the cheers to die down before going on with what might have been a political speech praising the people and the industry of their copper miners, the riches flowing out of the Mule Mountains, his great friendship with Judge DeWitt Bisbee, the promise Bisbee showed for the territory, and adding a half-dozen other hollow-sounding phrases that made Slocum wonder if Peake *was* running for office.

The governor of the territory was appointed, but that didn't mean Peake couldn't get out and make his stump speeches against the day Arizona became a state. Slocum doubted that would be anytime soon, but Peake might know more than even the clever, smart citizens of Bisbee that he addressed with such reverence.

As he spoke, a woman came from the car and stood behind him. She was several years younger and well-dressed, but Slocum couldn't take his eyes off the diamond necklace she wore. It had been a while since he had strayed to the other side of the law to hold body and soul together, but the sight of such a bodacious necklace made him think of larceny. The woman needed such a flashy piece of jewelry, he decided, because she was otherwise not much to look at. Not ugly—far from it—but not as pretty as Belle Wilson, and certainly far from Lily Montrechet's outstanding looks.

But this rather plain, mousy brunette was undoubtedly married to Norbert Peake and had access to his vast wealth. She reached out and laid a hand on the man's shoulder. The sunlight glinted off the large diamond ring, confirming Slocum's guess that this was Peake's wife. The railroad magnate impatiently brushed her hand from his shoulder and launched into an even louder encomium of Bisbee and its residents.

Anyone who rambled on with such praise wanted something. Slocum wondered what was in Bisbee that the railroad magnate could possibly desire so that he went to such fulsome lengths to get it. A man of his wealth need only buy what he wanted. The Copper Queen Mine ruled Bisbee with its output, but the gold mines were more profitable for smaller groups of miners. A few of those men might have become rich, but nothing compared to the obvious wealth sported by Norbert Peake and his wife just in jewelry.

It was another mystery, and one Slocum was not too intent on delving into right now. The rich made plans that were sometimes obscure to men of ordinary means. Right now, all Slocum wanted was to get to Yuma and find Cara. The woman had tried to kill him for no reason he could fathom. A faint hope flared in him that Cara had been responsible for Lily's death and could have killed him at the watering hole but, for whatever reason, had not. Later, in town, she had spotted him and come on to him to finish the job. This theory didn't ring true, and Slocum felt down in his gut that he was wrong, but Cara was his only hope right now to begin tracking Lily's murderer.

Lady Death, Wyman had called her. Could he have meant Cara? She was certainly treacherous enough, intending to shoot him in the same bed where they had made love. But then Wyman had also said Cara worked for Lady Death. Where was the truth? Slocum had to find Cara to discover that elusive commodity.

Slocum would find out soon enough. The sounds from the crowd were drowned out by the brass band playing more enthusiastically than in tune. Peake and his wife stepped down from the back of their railcar, and were escorted to a buggy draped with red-white-and-blue bunting. The band in the lead, the buggy rattled off with the cheering crowd following. Slocum felt an almost physical relief when the crush of people diminished, and he was left alone at the railroad depot.

"We're swingin' them cars round now, mister," called the ticket agent. "Get yer horse into the second freight car. Got three other nags takin' a ride, too, so be sure to secure the horse real good so it don't get spooked or tangle with the other nags." The agent turned to a man standing impatiently on the platform and spoke to him in a low voice. There seemed to be some disagreement, but the potential passenger finally handed over a few dollars in return for a ticket.

Slocum retraced his steps to Belle's house to fetch his horse. He considered sticking his head inside to see if the drug had worn off yet, but decided against it. Whatever scheme she had in mind had been derailed when he'd switched drinks. Slocum saw no reason to give her a second chance. He swung into the saddle and rode back to the depot, finding the proper freight car easily enough. The man who had argued with the ticket agent struggled to get his swaybacked horse into a stall in the car. The animal kicked against the back of the car, threatening to knock out a panel. The man was turned toward the horse, his full attention on keeping the skittish beast under control.

"Better get that horse settled down before the train gets rolling," Slocum said. "Otherwise, it's likely to hurt itself."

"Who cares?" the man growled as he worked to get his horse into the stall. He hadn't shaved in a few days, and his bloodshot eyes were filled with anger when he turned.

Slocum shrugged it off. Some men didn't have the sense God gave a goose. If the horse got caught after kicking out a panel, it could panic and break a leg. Then the horse wouldn't be any good at all, not that it looked as if it could carry a rider more than a few miles now without keeling over.

The man grumbled constantly, then stopped suddenly and stared at Slocum. He started to say something, but was cut off when the conductor poked his head into the car and yelled, "Git them horses all tied down good now. We're pullin' out in a minute or two."

"Done," Slocum said, swinging out and dropping to the

ground beside the conductor. Slocum looked back into the car and wondered at the other man's expression. It was as if he had seen a ghost, or maybe Heaven itself. His reaction was strange, but Slocum pushed it aside and talked to the conductor all the way to the passenger car. He turned to see the man jump to the ground from the freight car, catching his coat on a nail and ripping off a large patch. He grumbled some more about this, but probably wouldn't try to retrieve the missing patch within the few minutes they had since there were several other large holes in the threadbare coat. One thing Slocum did notice as the man tugged the coat around him was the shoulder rig he wore. The leather straps were clean and polished and the butt of the pistol sticking out from under the left arm looked new.

The man ran to the passenger car and rudely pushed past Slocum and the conductor, took the steps up to the small platform in a single leap, and settled down in the last row, arms crossed and glaring as if he was mad at the world. Slocum snorted in disgust as he walked past. The man had taken the spot Slocum wanted. At the rear of the car he could watch everyone else and have his back to a solid wall. Slocum went to the front of the car and slid across a hardwood seat to the window. The heat had already built to a furnace-hot intensity inside the car, so he lowered the window and caught a hint of arid breeze blowing across the desert. When the train started, he intended to close the window to keep the hot cinders from the engine's smokestack from coming inside and burning holes in his coat and skin.

Another five minutes passed and a dozen other passengers filed in, most choosing seats as far from the others as possible.

Slocum played a little game of figuring out who they were and where they were going. A woman and her small son were easy enough. They rode to Tucson, probably to visit family. A couple of miners and a peddler got into a poker game that would end badly for the almost-drunk snake-oil salesman. The rest scattered throughout the car were cowboys or businessmen, from the cut of their clothing. The only one Slocum couldn't hazard a guess about was the gent in the rear of the car, now pretending to be asleep, chin resting on his chest.

From the way the man shifted on the wood seat, he was far from asleep. If anything, he was watching everyone aboard more closely than Slocum. Ordinarily, this wouldn't bother Slocum unduly, but the shoulder holster and the well-kept gun carried by a man pretending to be the epitome of down-at-the-heels drifter hinted that trouble might be around the corner.

Slocum wedged himself into the corner formed by the seat and the railcar wall, and found a decent spot where reflections from the back of the car were mirrored in the upper window. Nobody was likely to sneak up on him as long as he maintained a vigil.

The car lurched and a loud clanging bell sounded as the engine backed up. Slocum saw that there was only the one passenger car, but the conductor made sure to hook up four more freight cars. Not so many passengers, more cargo. That suited Slocum fine.

The whistle sounded three times; then the train clanked and surged forward as the conductor made his way into the car.

"Ticket?" he asked, bored. Slocum passed over the fragment he had taken from Wyman's pocket. The conductor took it, frowned, and handed it back. "That one's been used. What are you trying to pull, mister?"

"Used? From Yuma?"

"From Yuma," the conductor agreed without a second thought. "I got to collect the fare in cash if you don't have a ticket."

"Sorry about that," Slocum said, handing the conductor the ticket purchased at the depot. The man grunted, punched it, and handed it back. He moved on, punching the tickets until he got to the rear of the car and confronted the man with the shoulder holster.

Slocum slumped in his seat to get the reflection just

right so he could watch. The conductor blocked much of the view, but Slocum saw the man was arguing over the ticket. The conductor took a letter from the man, held it up to read it, shook his head, handed it back, and argued a bit more with the man, who reluctantly passed over the ticket he had purchased. Slocum wished he was a fly on the wall to hear that exchange.

The conductor seemed satisfied with the ticket and went to the rear door, swinging around on the tiny platforms between cars to get into the one immediately behind the passenger car. Slocum reckoned that was a mail car. As this thought crossed his mind, he wondered about the surly passenger seated so close to the door leading back into the next car.

Maybe something valuable was being shipped. This was a gold-mining region, though there weren't many smelters capable of refining the ore to produce gold ingots. Slocum had seen all kinds of men commit robberies, and the one at the back of the car was as likely a suspect as any he had ever met.

It wasn't any of his concern, as long as the owlhoot intended to rob the train and not the passengers. Slocum had to smile at this. He had only the money he had taken from Wyman to show for all his misadventures. That would be slim pickings for any train robber.

Slocum dozed, the rocking of the train and the clanking of the steel wheels on the tracks soothing for him. He awoke a half hour later, rubbed his eyes, and winced. He had gone to sleep with his arm braced against the wall and exposed to the direct sunlight coming through the open window. Slocum realized he should have closed the window or rolled down his sleeve, but now it was too late. He winced at the sight of new blisters on already tender skin.

Getting to his feet, Slocum gripped the backs of the seats as the swaying train tried to throw him about. He needed to get Belle's jar of ointment from his saddlebags to tend his new burns and blisters. He walked down the aisle like a drunk until he got the hang of rolling with the motion

of the car. As he approached the shabbily dressed man at
the rear, Slocum saw him stiffen and turn, his hand slipping
under his coat to rest on the butt of his hidden pistol.

Slocum thought nothing of it. No one else had gone
back, and the owlhoot obviously was mighty nervous for
some reason. As Slocum passed him and opened the door
onto the platform between cars, he saw movement from the
corner of his eye. He turned slightly—and this was enough
to keep the man from braining him with the pistol barrel.
Sparks flew as the gun crashed into a metal support. Curses
followed.

Staggered and off balance, Slocum fell onto the tiny
platform and pulled the door shut behind him. The man's
gun was caught between door and doorjamb. Inexorably,
Slocum saw the muzzle being lowered and pointed toward
him. If he let go of the door, the man would get a clean
shot, and there was no way in hell Slocum could hope to
crush the barrel using only the metal frame and the wooden
door.

The man pulled the trigger, and a slug ripped past
Slocum's ear.

"What're you doing, you crazy fool?" Slocum shouted,
hoping his words carried over the noise of the rolling railcar and brought help. But who that might be, he couldn't
say. The conductor had vanished toward the rear of the
train, and probably would take long sips from a whiskey
bottle back in the caboose until they pulled into Tucson
and he had duties again. There might be a guard in the next
car, if his guess about the man being a robber going after a
valuable shipment was right.

But a second shot caused Slocum to wince. The bullet
grazed the arm that had been newly sunburned. The pain
doubled. Tripled. Slocum recoiled, and his grip on the door
handle slipped. The man flung the door open and pointed
his pistol squarely at Slocum.

"Got you now," he said. The man's intent on killing
Slocum was obvious. "This time you ain't got the conductor to hide behind."

Slocum kicked out hard as the train highballed around a curve in the otherwise-straight run of track. The combination of his boot hitting the man's leg and the way the car rolled caused the third shot to go wide by a mile. Not wanting to give the man another chance, Slocum twisted around furiously and grabbed a handful of coat. Pulling as he fell back onto the small metal platform drew the man forward. Then Slocum kicked him in the balls.

A dull *whuff*! escaped the man's lips, but he clung stubbornly to his pistol, instinctively knowing he was a dead man if he dropped it. Slocum pulled harder and rolled the man to one side so his head was dangling off the side of the platform. He grabbed the man's gun hand with his left, squeezed, and rolled his weight onto the struggling would-be killer.

"Dammit, drop the gun," Slocum grated out. "Why are you trying to kill me?"

This caused a surge of determination in the other man. He lifted Slocum bodily, but lacked the leverage to throw him off the train. Slocum went straight up and came straight down, his knee drawn in so he could jam it into the man's belly. A second gasping noise broke loose from his attacker's lungs, and Slocum felt the fight go out of the man.

Not taking a chance, Slocum lifted the man's gun hand and then slammed it down hard against the top step of the platform. The gun tumbled to the tracks and was caught under the steel wheels, crushed instantly by the prodigious weight of the train car.

"Why'd you try to kill me?"

"You got it all wrong. I thought you were going to kill *me*."

Whatever explanation Slocum had expected, this was not it. The moment of surprise caused him to relax his grip enough for the man to fight back. Although he had a bruised wrist from where Slocum had banged it against the metal step, the man packed quite a wallop with his right hand. Then he followed with an even more powerful left-handed punch that rocked Slocum.

Slocum kicked again and hit the man in the right hand. He screamed in pain as he clutched the injured arm. Slocum saw bright white bone poking through the skin now, and knew he had to take advantage fast. In the cramped space of the platform, he dragged himself to his feet, set his heels into the metal grating, and swung. Slocum's fist connected with the man's chin and snapped his head back. From the way the man's eyes glazed over and then rolled up in his head, Slocum knew the uppercut had done its job.

The man wobbled and began to topple backward off the platform. Slocum grabbed the man's coat, but the decrepit cloth tore free as the man toppled from the train. Left with nothing but a handful of ripped coat, Slocum stuck his head out around the side of the car and saw the man lying beside the tracks. Then the train rushed on and the man was left in the desert.

He might have been dead from the fall or simply unconscious, but he certainly was not going to try to kill Slocum again any time soon. Slocum looked at the fistful of fabric and felt the bulk to it. He began peeling away layers until he revealed a wallet. A smile came to his lips at this minor success. Flipping it open, Slocum turned grim when he saw the contents. A small shining gold badge inside proclaimed the bearer to be a railroad detective. A few dollars in greenbacks were tucked inside, too, but the badge told Slocum he had big troubles. He found the letter the man had shown both the ticket agent and the conductor and scanned it quickly. It was a short letter signed by Norbert Peake telling the reader of the letter to give the possessor all possible consideration. The railroad detective had obviously tried to use the letter to gain free passage from both the ticket agent and the conductor, and both had demurred.

Slocum folded the letter and stashed it, then tucked the wallet with its gold badge into his inside pocket, climbed up to the roof, and precariously made his way back to the freight car with his gear, applied Belle's salve to his new sunburn, and felt better for it. But he had to worry, just a little, about why a railroad detective had tried to kill him.

His horse refused to answer his questions, but Slocum didn't mind. He retraced his path back to the passenger car, now carrying one less passenger. Slocum settled down where the railroad detective had ridden, more secure but discontent.

13

Slocum pulled out the letter from the railroad detective's wallet and read it again, marveling at how cheap the man must have been. A letter from Norbert Peake authorized the bearer to "all courtesy" from Arizona Central Railroad employees, but nothing was said about free passage. Slocum decided that had been the bone of contention between the detective and the conductor earlier. The detective had demanded to ride without paying, but must have known this letter was worthless for that since he had purchased a ticket earlier.

Slocum fished out the ticket stub taken from Boots Wyman and stared at it. Why had Wyman stuffed it in his pocket if he and his partners had arrived from El Paso? They might have been in Yuma for some reason.

"Pardon me," Slocum said as the conductor made his way forward. "Where's the headquarters for the railroad?"

"Headquarters? You mean where Mr. Peake keeps his office? In Yuma."

"Thanks," Slocum said, wondering if this was important. Had Wyman, Dumont, and Prentiss gone to Yuma and been hired by Norbert Peake as detectives? Or were they simply what they seemed, bounty hunters looking for men wanted by the Arizona Central Railroad? The answers were in Yuma, a town Slocum had never much liked.

125

He stared out the train window as they rattled closer to the town perched on the east bank of the Colorado River. As they passed the penitentiary, he couldn't take his eyes off the tall gray stone walls with adobe buildings dotting the surrounding empty desert. Getting out of that prison was almost impossible. Before he knew it, Slocum heard the conductor bellowing that they were almost at the station in Yuma. Slocum tucked the railroad detective's wallet away securely in a pocket, and then settled his six-shooter at his hip. In spite of the specter of the Yuma Penitentiary, this was a wild, wide-open town. The unwary died fast here.

Slocum climbed off onto a depot platform indistinguishable from the one in Bisbee. He looked around, almost expecting to be met with a hail of bullets. With a snort of disgust at himself for such fanciful thinking, he went down the train and waited for one of the yard hands to cut open the wire holding the door of the stock car closed. When he had fetched the salve for his wound while the train was still rolling, he had climbed up onto the top of the car and dropped down inside through a small access hatch in the roof. Slocum now climbed in through the open door and gave his horse a lump of sugar he had been hoarding for such an occasion, then unfastened the ropes and led it from the car down a ramp.

Mounting, he looked around and decided Yuma didn't look too much like Bisbee, except for its railroad station. Bisbee was a thriving town, filled with energy and money flowing from its nearby mines. Yuma had the look of a sleepy border town. Or maybe the nearness of the penitentiary cast a pall over the people that kept them from laughing and smiling and looking alive as they went about their business.

Slocum rode slowly from the rail yard and down Yuma's main street. If anything, seeing the businesses here depressed him even more. A few saloons were open, but had scant customers inside in spite of it being almost sundown. He wondered if most of the saloon customers consisted of the gray-walled penitentiary's guards. Working in such a grim place could make any man turn to drink to forget, and the inmates weren't likely to partake of any of the rotgut being sold in town.

Riding back and forth didn't strike Slocum as being too productive. He dismounted and went into a doctor's office, waiting until the bespectacled, bald man looked up. It took a second for the doctor to realize Slocum was even there since he had been so lost in reading the magazine opened flat on the desk in front of him.

"Sorry," the doctor said. "I was thinking about a particularly vicious way of curing an even more vicious infection. What can I do for you?"

"A friend of mine came back to town a few days ago. A woman with a bullet wound in the belly." Slocum described the brunette the best he could, finishing with: "She has bright violet-colored eyes. You see them, you're not going to forget them." He wondered if he ought to go into more detail about moles and other imperfections in the woman's bare body that he had noticed while they had been making love. He decided against it, although the doctor probably wouldn't even comment on how he had come to know such intimate details.

"Don't remember seeing anyone like that," the doctor said, "but then if she was well enough to travel from Bisbee, as you said, there's no reason for her to see me. She'd be well on her way to healing."

"There might be the matter of money," Slocum said. "She's not got a lot." He considered offering the doctor a "fee" to see if this might loosen his tongue or improve his memory. All he had was a few coins, the gold piece taken from Wyman, and the few crumpled greenbacks in the railroad detective's wallet.

The doctor laughed harshly. "Danged near everyone in this town's in that situation."

"Even with the Arizona Central Railroad headquartered here?"

"I've got nothing against Norbert Peake," the doctor

said, obviously carrying a grudge in spite of his denial, "but he sucks money up like a horny toad sucks up black ants. Yuma's not a rich town because the only thing in the way of industry we've got is that damned prison. Excuse me," the doctor said, peering at Slocum over the tops of his spectacles, "but you're not a guard or administrator, are you?"

Slocum laughed. "Do I look like a guard?"

"Can't tell the difference between guard and inmate," the doctor said, turning testy.

"My friend's a right pretty woman. Where might I look for her?"

"Try a saloon. Or the red-light district on the other side of town. That's what you meant, isn't it, about her being pretty?"

"Is everyone in Yuma as cynical as you, Doc?"

"If they're not, they ought to be," the man said, turning back to his magazine in obvious dismissal. Slocum peered around a screen at the side of the room to see if anyone lay on the small bed behind. It was empty. The doctor might have been right about Cara's condition. If she was well enough to travel, even as easy a ride as it was on the train, she didn't need his undoubtedly expensive services.

Slocum stepped into the cold darkness. Though Yuma had streetlights up and down the block, none had been lit. Slocum hunted a little more for another doctor, in case Cara had avoided the first one he had come upon, but there seemed no one else with a shingle hanging out. Knowing that he might have missed one, Slocum stopped a few citizens and asked. Two denied there was any other doctor in town, but the third scratched his head, then pointed.

"Down yonder, I think. In the saloon at the end of the street. Leastwise, he claimed he was a sawbones."

Slocum thanked the man, who was more than a little drunk, and went to the saloon. Unlike most, called the Longhorn or the Emporium or some other grandiose name, this one had a simple painted sign that declared: WHISKEY.

Slocum paused in the doorway and looked inside. For a saloon, it was mighty quiet. Three customers were bellied up to the bar and talked in low tones. A card game went on at the rear, and a bored woman with more gray than brown in her hair stood by herself at the faro table, idly flipping cards onto the table and then cutting them back into a deck. She looked up with listless eyes and motioned for Slocum to come over. He did.

"You wanna buck the tiger?" she asked. "You don't know how to play faro, I'll tell you. It's not so hard."

"That's all right," Slocum said. He knew the rules, but preferred poker if he gambled. "You know a girl with brown hair and violet eyes? Striking expression. Real pretty."

The woman blinked as if the thought—any thought—was in desolate country within her head. She finally came to some sort of decision.

"Talk to Smitty. The barkeep."

"Thanks," Slocum said, not sure if this was the woman's way of getting rid of him or if there might be a nugget of information at the end of the trail. He went to the bar and waited for the handlebar-mustached bartender to notice him.

"Beer," Slocum ordered. "And some information."

"Beer's cheap. The information might cost you some. What do you want to know?" The barkeep idly polished a glass with a filthy rag as he studied Slocum closely. If the woman faro dealer stood around in a stupor, Smitty's brain turned this way and that checking all the angles.

"There more than one doctor in town? Heard tell one was here in this saloon."

"Yeah, that's right," Smitty said. "That's me. You don't look hurt none."

"You're a doctor?"

"Was. Got my medical degree back in Baltimore, but came West for my health."

Slocum wondered if Smitty meant he had come to drier climate for a lung condition, or if he'd had to leave Baltimore because of some botched operation and an irate family. Whatever it was, he had ended up behind a bar rather than taking patients in a surgery.

Looking around, Slocum had to laugh. This place was probably cleaner than most doctors' offices he had seen, and there was an almost limitless supply of anesthetic in the bottles behind the bar.

"Friend of mine got a bullet in the gut. Over in Bisbee," Slocum said, watching the barkeep closely for even a flicker of emotion. "Her name's Cara. Got violet eyes you can't forget if you look into them." Smitty wasn't reacting until Slocum got to the color of Cara's eyes. The way the man's mustache twitched told Slocum the doctor-turned-bartender knew Cara.

"Don't know about any bullet in the belly," Smitty said. "But I might know who you're talking about."

Slocum pulled out the few dollars he'd taken from the railroad detective's wallet. He placed those on the bar and pinned them down with the half-empty beer mug.

"Might be you can even tell me where to find her."

"You put the bullet in her?"

"It was an accident," Slocum said. It had been, almost. "I want to make it up to her."

"Yeah, right," Smitty said, but his eyes kept returning to the bills under the beer mug. "She works at Loosey Lucy's a couple blocks to the north."

"Whorehouse?"

"What else?" Smitty said with just a touch of sarcasm in his voice.

Slocum knew he wouldn't get any more information from the man and left the saloon. There was no reason for Smitty to bandy words or play cute, but for some reason he found it odd that Cara worked in a brothel. He hoped to find a reason for her attempt on his life, and if she were a soiled dove, getting the truth might be close to impossible. Such women learned to lie convincingly. Slocum had to tread lightly on questioning Cara about her actions as well as trying to find out if she actually knew the Lady Death that Wyman had mentioned.

As he walked down the street, leading his horse, Slocum turned over and over what Wyman had said. He might have made up a tall tale on the spot to keep from getting killed, but Slocum began to wonder about the timing of the shot that had robbed Wyman of his worthless life. It had come at the precise moment when he could have given details about Lady Death. Did that mean the woman had been lying in wait, her rifle trained on Wyman, listening to what he might say about her? And when he had started to spill his guts, she had plugged him?

Slocum just didn't know. He had too many questions and fewer people to ask. Why had the railroad detective attacked him on the train? He had never seen the man before in his life.

The streets turned darker, and Slocum had the sensation of being watched from all quarters. He walked steadily until he saw a hand-carved sign proclaiming a ramshackle house to be LUCY'S. There weren't likely to be other such establishments with the same name. Slocum made sure his six-shooter slid easily in his holster, then went to the door and knocked.

He heard footsteps inside and a locking bar being pulled back. The door opened to a frowsy-looking woman, hair in disarray and her clothing askew, who leaned against the doorjamb in a practiced manner, showing a little leg and bending forward so Slocum could see the swell of her bosoms.

"You lookin' for a good time?" she asked. Before Slocum could say a word, the harlot pushed off from the door and stared at him with wide eyes. She let out a screech like a hunting hawk and came at him, hands drawn into claws as she tried to scratch out his eyes.

"You son of a bitch!" the woman shrieked hysterically.

Slocum caught her wrists and swung her around. The unexpected attack left him bewildered. Did everyone in

Arizona attack first and then think about it later? Not that he gave them a lot of chance to do any thinking. Cara, at least, had let him bed her before she tried to murder him.

The woman squirmed about and kicked at his shins. Slocum winced whenever her slippers connected. The fronts of his legs were on the road to healing, but the sunburn still stung under her assault.

"Quit it," he said, shaking her. If anything, this provoked a renewed attack. The Cyprian tried to kick him in the groin, but Slocum was ready for this. Holding both her wrists in his left hand, he grabbed her leg and lifted, dumping her onto the ground. "Stop fighting. I'm not going to hurt you!"

For an instant Slocum thought his words had gotten through to the infuriated woman. But like a mad dog, she renewed her attack the instant he relaxed. She spat and kicked and clawed. Slocum stepped away, and she came at him on hands and knees, trying to bite him on the leg.

"Stop or I'll drill you," Slocum said, his six-gun coming to hand easily. He pointed it at her. To emphasize that he meant business, he cocked the pistol. The sound was enough to make even the most mindless of men intent on attacking him have second thoughts. Not this woman. She didn't care if she lived or died as long as she took Slocum with her.

As she scooted in the dirt toward him, he swung his pistol and clipped her on the side of the head hard enough to knock her flat. It was too much to think it would knock sense into her. The woman's rage transcended that.

She was groggy but still fighting.

"Leave her alone," came a new voice. "Haven't you done enough to her already?" An older woman stood in the doorway, her fists clenched.

"I never saw her before. What are you talking about?" demanded Slocum. "Has everyone gone crazy?"

"You're the crazy one, you garbage-eating pig," the madam said. "After what you did to her sister, you think you can waltz in here and—"

Past the woman down the long hall in shotgun house, Slocum saw Cara emerge from a room and look in his direction. The woman's violet eyes glowed with rage; then she turned and ran toward the back of the house.

"Wait!" Slocum pushed past the madam and thundered after Cara, only to crash into a mountain of a man who had been in the room with Cara.

"You ain't gonna hurt her no more," the man said.

Slocum knew the look of a bouncer when he saw it. This man was all muscle, and that included the area between the ears. That didn't make getting past him any easier. His shoulders were so wide they rubbed against the walls on either side of the corridor. If anybody could be called two ax-handles wide across the shoulders, it was this behemoth.

Slocum quickly considered the six-shooter still in his hand, and knew it would have no more effect on this giant than it had on the more frantic woman who was outside the brothel sobbing in the arms of the madam.

"She tried to kill me," Slocum said, stepping back. He gauged his distance and kicked for all he was worth. The short duration of getting ready for the kick was all the man needed to rush him. As a result, Slocum's kick landed on the man's steely hard upper thigh instead of where Slocum had aimed.

Slocum grunted as the man pushed him back off balance. Slamming hard into a door, Slocum bounced off and crashed into the one across the hall from it. This time he went through, taking the door and frame with him to land facedown on the floor. Behind he heard the bouncer growling like some ferociously wild animal. Instinct saved him. Slocum rolled to the left as hard and fast as he could, barely missing being crushed by the bouncer's body toppling down.

Kicking again, Slocum launched off the giant man's body and got his feet under him. The bouncer grunted and struggled to come to his hands and knees. Slocum had two choices. He could put a bullet behind the man's ear and kill him, or he could do what he did. Rearing back, Slocum launched another tremendous kick that ended on the huge man's chin. The bouncer's head snapped back, and he half-rose, then crashed to the floor.

Slocum didn't waste any time getting back to the hall. He saw both the madam and her crazy whore coming after him again. The madam held a wicked-looking knife and the other one had her fingers curved into claws that would put any bear to shame. Again, he considered shooting. At this range he couldn't miss, but he had no quarrel with them, even if they seemed to hate his guts.

Tearing toward the rear of the house, he shouldered his way through the back door and burst out into a yard filled with garbage and discarded junk from all over town. At the back door, the madam stood and shouted curses at him.

Slocum was willing to let her do that all night long, if she didn't pick up a gun and start shooting. The one he wanted was Cara.

She was nowhere to be seen.

14

Amid the garbage and the ruin, Slocum studied the ground the best he could to see if he could pick up Cara's trail. All he got was a headache from inhaling the stench of the rotting garbage. He circled around and came out on the street. To his left stood the whorehouse and his horse, unaffected by the goings-on both inside and out. Warily going to the horse, he mounted and tugged on the reins to get the balky animal moving. It seemed to want to stay a spell, but Slocum desired nothing more than getting the hell away from this madhouse.

He rode down the street, heading back toward the saloon where he had learned of Cara's whereabouts, but he took a side street when he saw a knot of men gathering ahead of him along the street. There was no reason they would have it in for him, but he would have said the same about the whore back at Lucy's. And the bouncer and the madam. Truth to tell, Slocum wasn't popular anywhere he went. Cara had tried to murder him, the railroad detective had, too, and people around Slocum died fast.

Lily Montrechet came instantly to mind.

He discounted Wyman, Prentiss, and Dumont, although they also pushed up daisies from shallow graves.

Slocum found himself fighting to remember why he was even in Yuma. He laughed without humor at the notion that

Lady Death was behind it all, as Wyman had tried to convince him. She was a phantasm floating beyond belief. Still, some expert marksman had killed Lily and Boots Wyman. The skill involved in each of those murders was remarkable, and Slocum thought both times the trigger had been pulled by the same person. But someone known as Lady Death? There was no proof.

For a while he had considered Cara in that light, but she had not even checked the derringer to be certain it was loaded before turning it on him. She seemed expert enough in using the small pistol, but there was a world of difference between a derringer and a Winchester rifle, shooting at point-blank range and hitting a target hardly the size of a silver dollar at a hundred yards.

Answers were what he needed most. Starting with Cara, he would get them. What she told him would determine his next move.

Slocum rode slowly up and down the streets of Yuma until dawn began poking pink and gray fingers into the sky. Unlike Bisbee, Yuma did not come alive with the promise of a new day. If anything, there was a dread that settled down like some vile net over the people coming out to open the stores and go about other business.

Nowhere among them did Slocum spot Cara. He wondered if she hadn't gotten off to a stable and taken a horse out of town after leaving the brothel. Slocum didn't cotton much to the idea of returning to Lucy's to find out more about Cara and where she was likely to run. He had hoped to find her once she hightailed it, but he was rapidly approaching the point of giving up. Then he got down from his tired horse, went into a café, and ordered breakfast. Somewhere during the second cup of strong coffee, he formulated a plan he should have followed right away. Cara knew Yuma; he didn't. He should have methodically gone to the stables, to saloons, to places where she might have taken refuge. Even the crusty old doctor might have an idea or two about where a young, pretty woman of the night might hole up if she was on the run.

Certainly Smitty the barkeep would know such things. And maybe the faro dealer. And Loosey Lucy.

Slocum stepped out, knowing the meal was the best thirty cents he had spent in quite a spell, stretched his tired muscles, then started making the rounds, going from one store to the next asking after Cara. Only when he went into the telegraph office did he strike paydirt.

"You remember seeing her?" Slocum asked the telegrapher. The man pushed his green eyeshades up and stared nearsightedly at Slocum. His hands burned from acid used in the telegraph batteries and his eyes watery, he looked like something that might have crawled out of the garbage pile behind Lucy's whorehouse.

"Can't fergit a looker like her. No, sir, not fergitin' her."

"Did she send a telegram this morning?"

"Nope. It was last night."

"Who'd she send it to?" Slocum asked.

"Cain't tell ya that. 'Gainst company policy."

Slocum saw that the telegrapher had little to boast of other than devotion to duty. He had to change his tactics a little.

"That couldn't be her, then. The telegram Cara sent would have gone out this morning."

"Last night. If she's the one, and I don't fergit a face like hers."

"You did, though."

The man snorted in contempt at such an allegation and dragged out a heavy ledger book. He opened it and ran his finger down the column until he came to the most recent telegram.

"You said her name's Cara? This is her 'gram. One o'-clock in the A.M., it was when she sent it. I know since I keyed it in all by my lonesome. Not any later 'n that, no, sir."

Slocum read upside down the best he could. The contents of the telegram weren't recorded in the ledger, but the recipient was and it startled him.

What was Cara sending to Norbert Peake?

"What's the rate to Bisbee?"

The telegrapher looked at Slocum through slitted eyes. He slammed shut the ledger and put it back under the desk.

"Why do you ask?"

"That's where Mr. Peake is right now, isn't it?"

"I wouldn't know nuthin' 'bout that." The man glared at Slocum. Having made all the enemies he needed for a lifetime, Slocum thanked the telegrapher and left. The more he found out, the stranger and more difficult to explain everything was.

He walked slowly along the Yuma streets, an eye peeled for Cara, but the violet-eyed woman was nowhere to be seen. Slocum slowly made his way back to the bar with the simple WHISKEY sign dangling outside it and glanced inside. There were about the same number of customers inside now that there had been the night before. So much for a thriving business.

Slocum walked in and sank into a chair, bone-tired. It had been too long since he'd had any sleep, but he couldn't let up now. Not unless he wanted Cara to get away from him.

"What'll it be, mister?" asked the waitress. She might have been the twin sister to the faro dealer from the night before. Other than that she had her hair cropped shorter, Slocum would have mistaken her for the dealer.

"Coffee, with a shot of whiskey in it," Slocum said, deciding to drink the coffee to stay awake and the whiskey to kill some of the pain in his body. The sunburn had died to a dull ache long since, but going so long without sleep was giving him the twinges. "And some information."

"We kin rustle up the coffee, but I ain't supposed to say nuthin' to no one 'bout anything."

"Cara," he said, watching her reaction.

"I need to ask Smitty. He don't like us gossipin' none."

"It's not gossip if you just tell what you know's true," Slocum said.

She shook her head and looked like a frightened rabbit.

"I already know a lot of it, anyway," Slocum said. "She

had it coming," he said, taking a shot in the dark. He saw the woman bristle, and a hint of flush came to her pallid cheeks. She stamped her foot and put her balled hands on her hips as she glared at him.

"How dare you say that? Nobody deserves to have their head run over by a train!"

Slocum fought to keep his surprise down.

"Cara? She's dead?"

"Cara? What's she got to do with this? I'm talkin' about Missy's sister, Leonore. She was all trussed up and put on the tracks and Mr. Peake's very own train ran over her head. The only way they could figger out who it was all headless and bloody was by her bracelet. Missy had given it to her a week before, for her birthday. She was only nineteen."

"Where'd this happen?"

"You said you knowed all about it. You know it was just outside of town, on the tracks goin' toward Tucson. Not three miles out." The waitress shuddered all over and the color that had come to her cheeks faded now. "It was real terrible."

"The Arizona Central Railroad?"

"What else?" The woman sounded even more bitter and tearful than before. "Mark my words, nuthin' in this whole damn territory happens without Norbert Peake knowin' all 'bout it."

Slocum sat for a moment, trying to digest everything he had heard.

"Missy works at Lucy's?" He remembered the woman who had come at him like a wildcat, trying to claw out his eyes.

"Where else? You oughta know her," the waitress said, coming closer and peering at him. For the first time he noticed how nearsighted she was. Anything beyond the tip of her bulbous nose must be a blur from the way she squinted so hard. "You go there all the time, don't ya, John?"

The use of his name startled him. "I just got into Yuma. I haven't been in this town in a month of Sundays."

"Liar," the woman said, almost spitting at him. "I recognize you now from what Missy said." She licked her lips and wiped away some of the tears from her slightly unfocused eyes. "Never liked Missy much. She can be a real bitch. Her sister, now, she was always real kind to me. Losin' Leonore was a tragedy. Why didn't you go and kill Missy 'stead of Leonore?"

A sudden noise caused the waitress to peer myopically over at the bar as Smitty rolled a beer keg in from the back room. The barkeep looked up, wiped his hands, reached under the bar, and came around with a bung starter. The way Smitty swung it, Slocum knew the irate bartender intended to drive it through the top of his skull.

"You got real nerve comin' in here. Lucy tole me what went on 'tween you and Missy. If I'd known it was you, I'd have taken care of you last night. You murderous son of a bitch!"

The barkeep lifted his mallet and started to swing, but Slocum had his Colt Navy out and pointed at the man's midriff. Smitty froze and looked down at the steady grip, the unwavering line between the muzzle of the six-shooter and his gut. He lowered the mallet but continued to glare.

"You have some nerve comin' in last night like you don't know nuthin'," Smitty said. "Get the hell out of my saloon right now. I don't cotton to your kind in here. Sooner have a nigger or an Injun in here than the likes of you!"

Slocum stood, his six-gun still centered on the man's belly. His finger twitched at the barkeep's outburst; then he backed away and left the saloon without another word. Out in the middle of Yuma's hot main street, Slocum simply stood and looked around. Had the heat made everyone in this town loco?

Missy obviously had mistaken him for the man who had killed her sister. But why was she passing the description around the way she was? Cara must be Missy's friend, and had mistaken him for the man they thought had killed the woman by putting her head onto railroad tracks and letting the train run over her. Slocum shivered in spite of the heat. That was a hell of a way to die.

It didn't answer all the questions he had, but it went a ways toward explaining some. He was being confused with a woman-killing no-account skunk. But Lily had died from a single shot when the killer could as easily have plugged Slocum in the back. If Lily's death was an accident, why hadn't there been more shots since he must have been the intended target? And someone had made a habit of murdering the men he ran down before they could talk.

There was a trail of blood behind him, and Slocum vowed to shed a little more. If only he could figure out who to kill.

He went to his horse and swung into the saddle. The anguished neighs told him the horse was tired and deserved a rest. There just wasn't time, and this wasn't the place. Slocum saw Smitty and the waitress in the doorway of the saloon, glaring at him. The waitress vanished. Slocum didn't have to be a mind reader to know she was hightailing it for Lucy's whorehouse to tell the madam what had just happened. That would bring Missy and the bouncer and more trouble than Slocum wanted to deal with at the moment. He was not too keen on the notion of killing people who mistook him for someone else.

He put his spurs to the horse's flanks and trotted from town, ignoring the aggrieved sounds the horse made as they left Yuma behind. Slocum turned his horse's face toward the east and began a long curving route that eventually brought him to the Arizona Central Railroad tracks. He lifted one leg and hooked it around the saddle horn, bending forward slightly to look both directions along the steel rails. Missy's sister had been killed somewhere out here. Slocum wasn't sure what he would find, but answers had to be gleaned somehow. If he stayed in Yuma much longer, he was likely to get a bullet in the back.

Judging distances, he guessed Yuma lay a mile to the west. He doubted anyone would tie a woman to the tracks too close to town, fearing she might be discovered before the train did its dirty work. In his gut he had the feeling that the man who had murdered Missy's sister was one mean hombre and had wanted to torture her a spell. Lashing her to the tracks so her ear could pick up the vibrations of an approaching train was one hellacious way of torturing her. She would know for long minutes that her death was hurtling toward her and be unable to do anything.

"He had her facing Yuma," Slocum said. "So she could see the train coming and make her fear all the greater." He was developing quite a dislike for the man who had killed Leonore, but with it came new questions. Why had the killer been so vicious? This wasn't a crime of passion, but one well thought out and diabolical.

If it had happened the way Slocum imagined. He wiped sweat from his forehead, settled his hat to shield his eyes from the glare, and drew up his bandanna to mop even more sweat as he rode eastward along the tracks. It could just be that he was entirely wrong and that the woman had fallen and been killed. No torture, no vindictiveness.

He didn't buy that for an instant. The folks in Yuma were too worked up for it to have been an accident.

Riding slowly long enough for the sun to warm his back and get out of his eyes, he studied the rails for mile after mile. Then he saw a pair of coyotes scuffling and pawing at the tracks. They reared up and growled at him as he neared, but he saw no trace of a body. After the coyotes reluctantly abandoned their hunt, Slocum dismounted and examined the stretch of tracks they had so jealously guarded.

The rails were shiny and clean, but then it had been a week or two since the woman had been killed. The passage of trains along those tracks would erase any evidence. The wood ties, in spite of being dipped in creosote, gave Slocum his proof. Red stains stretched from one side of the tracks to the other, as if someone's head had been severed by a train highballing it along this long stretch.

He knelt and put his ear down on the tracks. No sound, no vibration, but he could see a far piece. This would be the spot a vicious man would tie a woman he wanted to torment before she died horribly. Slocum found strands of rope from a lariat caught between the rail and tie. Blood had soaked into the rope, too.

He stood and stared. This was the spot where Missy's sister had died. So why did everyone from Cara to Missy to a barkeep at a cheap saloon think he had anything to do with her death?

15

"I'll be damned," came the cold voice. "It's true. Murderers do come back to the scene of their crime."

Slocum turned and started for his six-shooter, but froze when he saw the huge bores of a double-barreled shotgun pointed squarely at him. For a moment all he could see were those two big tubes of death; then he forced himself to look at the man holding the weapon. A silver star hammered from a Mexican silver ten-peso coin hung precariously on the man's vest.

"You the Yuma marshal?" Slocum guessed. "There's no need for you to point that thing at me."

"Well, now, I reckon that's where we ride different trails," the man said. His finger rhythmically tapped the double triggers. Slocum hoped the shotgun didn't have a hair trigger. The nervous lawman would blow him in half by accident.

"I wasn't in Yuma long enough to do anything that'd get the law on my trail," Slocum said. For once this was true. Other than the fight at the whorehouse, he had been an upstanding citizen and hadn't broken a single law. No court would convict him of assault on the bouncer. The man had tried to kill him with his bare hands. If anything, Slocum ought to get a medal for his restraint in not filling his ugly carcass full of holes.

"Not this time, but before, John, before you were here long enough to get into all manner of trouble." The marshal's shotgun barrels flickered down toward the railroad tracks and came back to Slocum's chest.

"How'd you know my name?"

"Word gets around fast, not that it's been so long, when you think about it," the marshal said. "Now, I was never too fond of Leonore Zemansky because of how she hung out with the wrong folks like she did, but her sister Missy is one fine woman."

"Makes you the opposite of the waiter girl in Smitty's saloon," Slocum said.

"None of your sass, boy," snapped the marshal. "I need to clap some irons on you so we can get back to jail. You're gonna love the Yuma jail. It's like one of them fancy health spas you hear 'bout up at Manitou Springs in Colorado compared to the penitentiary outside town. You'll be pleading for me to keep you on instead of shipping you out to those vicious bastards, mark my words."

Slocum knew he could never stand to be penned up in the Yuma Penitentiary. Better to die at the marshal's hand here and now. But the same questions nagged him that had before.

"How did you know my name's Slocum?" he asked.

"Slocum? What are you going on about? You said your name was John."

"John Slocum," he said.

"You lyin' pile of cow flop," the marshal said, his anger breaking through his professional pride at having caught a criminal. "That's not your name."

"Has been since I was born in Georgia," Slocum said.

"Don't know about where you was born. Don't care, either. You're John Backus."

"Backus?" For a moment Slocum tried to remember where he had heard the name; then it came to him. Boots Wyman had mentioned that name in front of the tent saloon in Bisbee. Slocum had tried to place anyone named Backus and had failed, except for one gent years ago.

"Don't know why you'd kill an innocent young girl like Leonore the way you did. Well, she wasn't that innocent, maybe, not working for Miss Lucy close to a year and all, but you didn't have no call to tie her to the tracks the way you did. That was plumb mean."

"I didn't even hear about her death until a few hours ago," Slocum said. He saw his protests meant nothing to the marshal. The man had it in his head that anyone poking around into Leonore Zemansky's death had to be the one responsible for her murder.

"A likely story."

"Why would Cara send a telegram to Norbert Peake?" Slocum asked.

"No reason," the marshal said, but he hesitated before speaking. "What's that got to do with anything?"

"There's more going on than appears," Slocum said. He quickly related how Cara had tried to kill him, how Lily Montrechet had been shot from ambush, anything else that he thought might sway the marshal. After a few minutes, Slocum saw nothing was going to convince the lawman. Reluctantly, he let the lawman pluck the Colt from his holster and get him onto his horse for the ride back into Yuma.

Slocum kept looking in the direction of the Yuma Penitentiary, wondering how much trouble he was really in. The marshal obviously thought he was someone named John Backus, but proving he was not could be hard.

"Anybody likely to really know this Backus fellow?" Slocum asked. "I must look enough like him to confuse Cara and Missy Zemansky. But I'm not the man they think I am."

"Well, now, Mr. Backus, or whatever you're calling yourself right now, they're about the only folks who have seen him."

"Might be they haven't seen him at all but just heard him described by Leonore. If he was romancing her, might be Lucy saw him up close."

"Lucy don't see much of anything up close, 'less it's a stack of greenbacks. Never saw a woman, even a madam, so intent on raking in the money. She don't care who sees her girls as long as they pay. And that's between her and her hookers."

Slocum saw no way out of this. The people who could identify him as not being John Backus were the ones pointing fingers in his direction. The confusion of first names didn't help, either. He reckoned Cara had identified him from Missy's description and when he had answered to the name, she had jumped to conclusions, never asking if his last name was Backus.

He touched the pocket where he still carried the railroad detective's wallet and badge. A few minutes' consideration told him it would be worse to claim to work for the Arizona Central Railroad than to hope the marshal never saw the identification. Explaining how he had come by a working detective's wallet would be hard, especially since Yuma was the home office for the Arizona Central Railroad. All the marshal need do was send a deputy to Norbert Peake's office and ask. Then Slocum would be in even more trouble.

Whatever he did had to be soon. They rode into the middle of Yuma, heading for the calaboose. Once the cell door clanged shut behind him, Slocum knew his next stop would be either the penitentiary at the edge of town—or worse.

He rubbed his sweaty, gritty neck and knew it could have a hemp rope fitted around it for Leonore Zemansky's murder. As he moved, he felt a hardness in another pocket. His heart almost skipped a beat when he realized this was Cara's derringer. He had pulled it back in Bisbee when it looked as if he might have to take down Sheriff Yarrow, then had tucked it into his pants pocket when he had lit out after Wyman. But the tiny pistol wasn't in a position where he could draw it easily and get the drop on the marshal.

Slocum looked around, trying not to seem too concerned, hunting for any chance to escape. In a flash he saw it and took it. Stumbling from a saloon came a cowboy waving two six-guns around in the air. One was already empty and the hammer kept falling on empty chambers. But the other was loaded. The drunk fired it.

Slocum let out a shriek of pure pain and toppled from horseback. He crashed hard to the ground, thrashed about a moment, then lay on his side in the dust.

"Son of a bitch!" cried the marshal. The lawman jumped from horseback and waved his shotgun around. The drunk had already been grabbed by two other saloon customers and wrestled to the ground. "Hold that varmint. I'll be there in a minute. Son of a bitch shot my prisoner."

He knelt beside Slocum and rolled him over. Slocum held the derringer pointed directly at the marshal's belly. The lawman froze, realizing how close he was coming to getting a slug in the chest. Slocum reached out, grabbed his Colt from the marshal's belt, and had it cocked and jammed into the man's belly before the surprised lawman could even call out.

"I'm in a world of trouble, Marshal," Slocum said. "I'm not the one who killed Leonore, but there's no way I can prove that."

"Prove it by giving me the gun, Backus."

"The name's Slocum," he said, "and you just convinced me what I have to do. Get to your feet real slow, and we'll go into the jailhouse."

"All I have to do is give a shout. I got deputies all over town who'll come running."

"Do it and you'll force my hand. I don't want to kill you. I've got no gripe with you, but you'll never know that if you raise your voice."

Slocum got to his feet, scooped up the marshal's shotgun, and stayed close with his six-shooter jammed into the marshal's back and the derringer in his left hand down at his side, should he need to bring even more firepower to bear. They went into the adobe jail. The instant relief from the sun caused Slocum to sag just a mite, but he watched the marshal close enough to step back as the man tried to whirl around and bat the gun away. By the time the marshal had finished his turn, he was still facing the deadly six-shooter. Slocum added the derringer to convince the man of the folly of further resistance.

"I mean it, Marshal. I don't want to hurt you, but I will if you force me."

"That's what all the killers say, isn't it? Always somebody else forcing you to kill."

"Into the back," Slocum said, pointing to a heavy barred door leading to the cells. He grabbed a key ring off a hook and herded the marshal ahead of him. A quick look showed six empty cells.

"Looks like you get your pick, Marshal. Which is the most comfortable?"

"You won't find any mercy, Backus. I'll clap you in shackles and *then* lock you up. You'll never see the light of day once I get you—"

Slocum used his six-shooter to buffalo the marshal. He laid the long barrel alongside the man's head just hard enough to knock him out. Slocum had hit plenty of men, and had even killed one this way, but the marshal had a hard head. There hadn't even been any bones broken. Wasting no time, Slocum dragged the lawman into a cell and quickly tied him up with strips torn from the blanket. Then Slocum gagged him and secured him to the now-bare cot. He studied his handiwork, stepped from the cell, and locked it.

"That'll keep you out of my hair for a spell," Slocum said, hoping the deputies the marshal had bragged on wouldn't bother returning until sundown or later.

He tossed the keys on the marshal's desk and opened the outer door to cast a wary glance. Across the street two men sat beside the drunk who had fired off his six-shooter, sharing a bottle with the cowboy. From this vantage point, Slocum couldn't see much of the street, so he stepped out boldly, as if he had been visiting the marshal's office on business that had been successfully concluded. Nobody had noticed his earlier tumble from the horse, or if they did, they didn't give two hoots and a holler about it.

If he had any sense, Slocum knew he should get on the horse and ride like the wind for California or Oregon or someplace the hell away from Arizona Territory. But there were questions to be answered. He had yet to figure out who had killed Lily or why. Right now, just finding the owlhoot who had murdered her would be good enough. Let the reasons for her death go by the wayside and devil take the hindmost.

He should leave Yuma, but he didn't. Slocum rode for the railroad office down by the train yards. Everything kept coming back to the Arizona Central Railroad, for some reason. Leonore had been killed on the company's tracks, and the railroad detective had tried to kill him on the way here from Bisbee. Having run out of other sign to follow, he decided boldness was his only trail.

Whatever he did, he had to do it quick. When the marshal got out of his cell, he would be madder than a wet hen and might not let any recaptured prisoner live to stand trial, even for murder.

Finding the Arizona Central Railroad headquarters proved easy enough. Slocum simply rode in the direction of the rail yard and went to the biggest, finest building in the area. A three-story brick building with flags flying atop an even taller flagpole told him where the money and power rested. Slocum slid from the saddle, then walked up the broad steps to the tall double doors leading into a marble-floored lobby. He hesitated as he looked around. A man behind a desk to the right looked up.

"Can I help you, mister?"

Slocum wasn't sure what to say. He had come here with no clear plan in mind and was rushed into saying something. To turn and leave would only draw unwanted attention to himself.

"I'm looking for John Backus. He around?"

The man's expression froze.

"Who's askin' after him?"

Slocum reached into his pocket and dropped the railroad detective's wallet on the desk in front of the clerk so that it popped open to reveal the small gold badge.

"Sorry, sir, didn't recognize you." The clerk stood and took the wallet with the badge. "I'll be right back."

"What about Backus?"

"Don't worry about that, sir," the clerk said. But Slocum did worry. Something in the man's face told the real story. He had recognized either the badge by its number or the wallet and knew Slocum wasn't a railroad detective.

The instant the man ducked into a door leading to a long corridor vanishing into the west wing of the building, Slocum headed for the double doors. He listened to his gut when it told him he was running not only from the marshal, but the Arizona Central Railroad now.

"Stop him! Stop him!" came the cry. Slocum surged forward and hit the double doors at a dead run. By the time he reached the bottom steps, bullets were flying. Three men with the look of railroad detectives emerged from the doors and fired their pistols at him, pistols similar to the one the detective who had attacked him on the train had used.

Whipping the reins around, Slocum used the horse as a shield for a few paces, then vaulted into the saddle using the forward momentum to propel him up and around. He kept his head low, but the small-caliber bullets fell far short. If they had used rifles, he would have been dead by now, but luck held for him again. Whether it was good luck remained to be seen. He had hoped to find out something more about John Backus before stirring up a hornet's nest. He had obviously failed.

He considered heading out of town, going back to Bisbee to finish nosing around for Lily's killer, but from the number of men rushing from the railroad office building, he knew he would have a full-scale posse on his trail before sundown. They would spot him right away in the desert. He had to blend into the Yuma population, at least until he could get supplies together for the long ride back to Bisbee. This time of year, or at any time, crossing such a desert was a dangerous undertaking, even with suitable water and food riding in his saddlebags.

Right now Slocum had nothing.

16

Slocum knew he was riding into the teeth of a hungry beast by not leaving Yuma. The marshal would be found sooner or later and would have a posse out after Slocum in a flash. Riding slowly past the jail put Slocum's nerves on edge, but there wasn't any ruckus from the building. The marshal hadn't been discovered yet. Slocum kept riding, turned off the main street, and stayed on smaller streets, hardly more than alleys in some cases. This gave him the chance to sort through all that had happened and to figure out a plan of action.

At the bottom of the heap right now was finding Lily's killer. More important was clearing up the confusion between him and this Backus fellow. And on top looking down forlornly from the summit of that mountain of woe was the need to stay alive. Simply staying in the saddle helped in one respect. If he was riding along, apparently heading to some destination, nobody paid him any notice. He didn't want to go into a saloon or other place where the cardsharps and gun-handlers were always on the lookout for suckers. It would take only an instant for word to circulate how the marshal was hunting for him and for the gamblers to get the drop on him. The reward alone would make it worth their while.

But the problem with such a nomadic solution to his

immediate problem for concealment lay in that he could not do it forever and eventually had to find someone to answer his questions. He let his horse drink its fill at a water barrel, then went into a mercantile and poked about, buying a few items he would need for his ride across the desert to Bisbee. When he left Yuma. When. Slocum made sure he had enough food and water, and then there was nothing more to do but get out and rub elbows with the citizens of Yuma.

"What's that?" asked the clerk. Slocum looked up. He reached for his six-shooter without realizing it.

"Sounds like a crowd outside," Slocum said. He knew what that probably meant. Going to the store window, he looked out and saw the marshal haranguing a tight knot of angry-looking men. Two or three sported badges, but these deputies were in the minority.

"Got ourselves a criminal on the run, from the sound of it," the clerk said, shaking his head. "Marshal Tennent ain't got the sense God gave a goose."

"What do you mean?"

"This ain't the first prisoner that's escaped from the jail. Imagine that. We got the toughest penitentiary in the whole danged country out there in the desert, and the worst city jail anywhere right down the street. One they can't ever get out of, and the other leaks like a sieve." The clerk shook his head.

Slocum listened to the marshal offering a reward of a hundred dollars. That was enough to bring bounty hunters from all over the territory, thinking it would be easy money. For a moment he considered Wyman, Prentiss, and Dumont. They had worked as bounty hunters, but they were anything but capable. And they were all dead.

Slocum pushed such thoughts away. The past was done. He had to look to the future or end up in a boneyard outside town. Surviving the next few hours would be a chore.

Unless. . . .

"Fourteen dollars and two bits," the clerk said, totaling Slocum's purchases. It took about all the money he had left, but Slocum wasn't complaining. The clerk didn't seem in the least suspicious.

"That reward the marshal offered," Slocum said.

"A princely sum, a hundred dollars. Wish I could take time away from work. I'd go try to get me a piece of it. That's more than I make working here for two danged months. More!"

"Does he let anybody join up? Would I have to be deputized to get into his posse?"

"You're not from around here. I can tell. Anybody that's got a mind to can join the hunt. With other folks or not. If you go out with a bunch of others, though, you got to share even-Steven. Now and then somebody escapes from the big prison down to the south. Then it's more of a party to find the body and the reward's nowhere near as lucrative. Nobody gets across the desert without a whale of a lot of preparation. Like the food you bought. Finding dead bodies that've been out in the sun for a week or more's no Sunday picnic, believe you me."

"Thanks," Slocum said, not wanting to make too much of an impression on the clerk. If the reward energized an entire town, somebody would be in here asking questions before much longer. Slocum wanted to be clear long before then, but the idea in the back of his mind kept rolling over and over. Running like a scalded dog wasn't in his nature, but taking such an outsized risk was foolish.

He did it anyway.

Slocum went to the rear of the crowd and nudged the man next to him. "When does the hunting begin?" he asked.

"Anytime now. The deputies are leading separate posses. The marshal's takin' one on out hisself."

"What about those men?" Slocum saw a small knot of men standing beside the marshal, looking grim and not a one sporting a badge. The very similarity of their expressions warned him he wasn't going to like the answer.

"Them? Them there's detectives for the railroad. Don't

rightly know what this gent done, but he's riled Norbert Peake and his bullies, too."

"What's the name of the owlhoot we're hunting?" Slocum asked.

"The marshal said his name was Backus. John Backus. Tall fella,'bout your height." The man squinted at Slocum and asked suspiciously, "You're not him, are ya?"

Slocum laughed and hoped it didn't sound too forced.

"Not my name. What do you think's the best way of finding this Backus?"

"You think I'm gonna show my hand to somebody like you?"

"Like me?" This took Slocum aback.

"You're one of the posse, too. A hunnerd dollars is a lot juicier than fifty, now, ain't it?"

"Reckon so," Slocum said, relieved. The man was greedier than he was observant. The best Slocum could tell, Marshal Tennent had given a general description that might be about anyone in Yuma, other than for the height. Slocum was a six-footer, something rare on the range. Just to be sure, he slouched a little, pulled up his bandanna so it hid part of his face, and moved away from the man intent on finding John Backus for the reward. Slocum stopped a few feet from the railroad detectives. When they moved, he followed. It struck him that they probably had a better idea where to hunt in Yuma than the marshal.

The detectives stayed in their tight group and trooped off down the street, a few curious onlookers trailing. None of this bunch had any intention of sticking with the detectives, though, and most of them slowly fell away to get on with their own hunt. Slocum's intentions were different, though. He wanted to see who the detectives questioned because these were likely to be people he needed answers from himself.

At a cross street, two of the detectives continued along the main street while the other two went right. Slocum hesitated, then followed the ones taking the smaller street since they headed in the direction of Loosey Lucy's. He pulled his bandanna up a little more when he passed the saloon where Smitty tended bar inside, then slowed his pace as the detectives stopped in front of a pharmacy. They took time to roll themselves cigarettes. The blue smoke drifted back to where Slocum had paused to sit down on the boardwalk. His nose wrinkled and he tried to remember the last time he had had a good smoke. He couldn't.

He wondered what was going on, but then saw what the men waited for. Coming along from the opposite direction, limping as he came, his right arm in a sling, was the railroad detective who had tried to kill Slocum on the train.

"You havin' any luck?" asked the detective closer to the injured one.

"I found her. What about you?"

"Naw, nuthin'. The man's like dust. He just faded away and there's no findin' him. Yet."

"Get on back and tell the marshal to double the reward, if that'd help."

"What're you going to do, Carl?"

The injured detective reached out clumsily with his left hand, took the cigarette from the man's mouth, and puffed on it. A second satisfying drag, and then he handed it back.

"I'm gonna have a heart-to-heart talk with her. It might be a chore if I have to beat what I want out of her, but I'll do it." He made swinging motions with his injured right arm. The other two detectives laughed. Slocum leaned back and got into shadows when the two men trooped back past him without so much as a glance in his direction.

Slocum got to his feet and trailed the detective the others had called Carl, trying to avoid being seen as he slipped through the gathering darkness. Carl made no effort to look around as he plodded along with single-minded determination toward Lucy's brothel. Guessing the railroad detective's destination helped Slocum keep from being seen. By the time Carl reached the front door, the bouncer and Lucy herself stood outside.

Nobody looked pleased.

"Got to talk to her, Lucy. You know that."

"You're not gettin' by, Carlotti," the madam said firmly. "Cara's been through enough. Her and Missy both have been drug through knotholes backwards. It's time I put my foot down and saved them more misery."

"You know what's goin' on. The whole damn territory's gonna be ripped apart if this goes any farther. Don't make me come back with my boys to talk to her. They don't have my . . . gentle ways."

Lucy snorted in disgust. "Missy's been all tore up inside ever since Leonore died like she did."

"Backus did it. You know that."

Something about the railroad detective's tone put Slocum on guard. Carlotti knew more than he was telling the woman—and it was a world more than she knew.

"He was just followin' orders," Lucy said bitterly. "Leonore didn't deserve to end up tied to the tracks like that."

"I need to talk to Cara. No need to trouble Missy none. Not right now." Carlotti looked up at the bouncer, as if estimating what it would take to knock him down. Slocum knew firsthand it wouldn't be easy, even if the detective had both hands in good condition.

"Go on in, Carlotti. Don't be long. This is a business, you know."

"Thanks, Lucy. Here's a little something for you and the big fella." Carlotti clumsily pulled out a wad of greenbacks, and peeled off a few and passed them over to the madam. Lucy took the money with ill grace, passing a single bill to her bouncer, then began counting what the detective had given her.

Carlotti pushed past and went into the shotgun house, obviously acquainted with the layout. He went to a room to the left. Slocum hurriedly circled the house and peeked into one window after another until he found the right one. The window was raised to allow in the faint evening breeze, giving him a perfect view into the room.

Cara sat on a small cot, dressed only in frilly undergarments. She looked up at Carlotti. From the set to her bare shoulders and the way she shrank from him, there was no love lost between them.

"I tried, dammit," she said. "It's not my fault he got away like he did."

"The boss isn't going to like it, Cara. You said you had him in Bisbee."

"He's good. That's how he killed Leonore so easy. He talked her out of here and the next thing you know, Missy's burying her without a head."

"How smart can he be?" scoffed Carlotti. "He was dumb enough to become her lover."

Slocum wondered who they were talking about. From the way Carlotti spoke, he had sent Cara to Bisbee. Slocum wasn't sure why she had tried to kill him, other than the description of this John Backus was general enough to fit him, too.

"You weren't any luckier killing the stupid bastard than I was," Cara said sharply. "Look what he did to you on the train." She laughed. Carlotti crossed the room in one long step and slapped her hard across the face, knocking her flat onto the cot.

"Hold your tongue, you stupid whore. I don't know why I ever trusted you to kill Backus. I wasn't able to get over there and do it myself, but I coulda run him to the ground with enough men. But no, I sent you."

"There was a whole passel of men after him, and they're all planted in the Bisbee potter's field now," Cara said, wiping away blood from a split lip. "That Boots Wyman was supposed to be a real gunslinger. Him and his two partners. They're dead. All three of them. Backus killed 'em all!"

"Good riddance," Carlotti said. "They only got in the way. What we have to do now is find Backus and kill him. Maybe capture him, torture him a little, put his head on the tracks, and let the train squash his brains like he done to Leonore."

Slocum frowned at such a fate since they thought he

was this Backus. He had no intention of ending up like that.

"Hell, Carl, you got no imagination. Tie his balls to the track, then take the rest to Mr. Peake. I doubt even that'd satisfy the vindictive old windbag."

"Don't talk that way about Mr. Peake. He's a good man, and he's been done wrong. We got to correct that."

"Why can't he do his own dirty work? If I didn't love you, Carl, I swear, I'd walk away from all this. Hell, I'd get on that damned iron horse and ride it as far as it'd take me. El Paso. San Antonio. The Gulf of Mexico. I don't care." She reached out and grabbed Carlotti's good hand and held it. "Let's you and me forget this crazy blood feud. Nobody's gonna win it, Carl. Not us, certainly not them."

He yanked back from her and glared.

"You're nuthin' to me, Cara. I thought I could trust you, but you showed that I can't."

"Carl!" The woman got to her feet, but he shoved her back and slammed the door behind him as he stormed out. Slocum knew he wouldn't have a better chance at talking to Cara than this. He slithered over the window ledge and into the room. The noise he made caused Cara to spin around. Her hand went to her mouth as she gasped. Before she could open the door or even call out, Slocum crossed the tiny room and clamped a hand over her mouth.

"Keep quiet," he ordered. He felt droplets of blood from her split lip oozing between his fingers. Easing off on his grip, he waited to see if she would call out. When she didn't, he released her.

"What are you doin' here? Ever'one in town's huntin' for your scalp."

"I noticed," Slocum said dryly. "I eavesdropped just now." He had to grab her as she tried to bolt and get away. The door stuck just enough to keep her from making an easy escape. Slocum slammed his palm against the flimsy door panel to hold it shut.

"You'd better clear out," Cara said, backing away. She

tripped and sat down hard on the cot. He read the fear in her eyes, although she tried to appear calm.

"You tried to kill me because Norbert Peake told you, right?" Slocum said. The woman nodded, her violet eyes brimming with tears. "Who's this John Backus that a powerful man like Peake couldn't have men like Carlotti do it for him?"

"Mrs. Peake had him kill Leonore because she was fooling around with Mr. Peake and she didn't cotton much to it."

Slocum stared at the woman for an instant. "Mrs. Peake told Backus to kill her husband's mistress? She thought that would stop him from stepping out behind her back?"

Cara shrugged. "Who knows what those people think? But Norbert Peake hired me to kill John Backus. From the description Carl gave me, I thought you were him." Violet eyes fixed on Slocum. "You're not spinnin' a tall tale with this, are you, John? You're really Slocum and not Backus?"

Slocum was thinking hard and only nodded. He didn't hear the door creak open until it was too late.

The muzzle of a small pistol poked through. Cara cried out, and Slocum spun, drew, and fired at the same instant a puff of smoke billowed from the other gun. Cara gasped and fell back onto the cot, deader than a doornail.

Slocum fired through the door panel, sending splinters flying throughout the small room, but Cara's killer was long gone.

From the appearance of the pistol and the clumsy way it was wielded, Slocum knew who had gunned down the soiled dove. He set out after Carlotti to settle the score. For Cara. And for himself.

17

Slocum had no love for Cara, not the way she had tried to kill him. In the end he thought of her about the same way he did of Wyman and his partners. They were bounty hunters and nothing more. Maybe Cara had turned the derringer on him because of love for Carlotti, devotion to Norbert Peake, or anger toward John Backus for killing her friend. Reasons didn't matter to Slocum. None of them.

But he didn't like Carlotti getting away with shooting the woman down simply because he had missed a shot at Slocum's back.

In the corridor outside the room, Slocum looked toward the front door and saw the mountain of a bouncer lumbering along, coming to see what had provoked the gunfire. Slocum doubted Carlotti had gone past the man, and turned toward the back of the house. The door stood open at the end of the hallway, possibly betraying where Carlotti had fled. Slocum wished there had been time to check each of the rooms. He imagined the railroad detective sneaking into one of them, even an occupied one, and lying in wait. He might have to silence the room's occupants, but that wouldn't be hard.

Slocum felt the hackles rising as he passed each door in turn at a dead run, then burst out into the night. The full stench of the garbage heap hit him like a hammer blow, but he caught sight of a shadow vanishing through the piles of rubbish and headed in that direction. Carlotti couldn't be too far ahead of him. And he wasn't.

The detective ran with his head down, his good arm pumping as he tried to make as good a speed as he could. His injuries kept him from making much progress. Slocum skidded to a halt, raised his pistol, and drew a bead. With a slow squeeze on the trigger, he got off a shot that sent Carlotti stumbling face-forward into the dirt. Slocum had shot enough men in his day to know when a shot felt right. He had only winged Carlotti.

"Get to your feet or I'll shoot you where you lay," Slocum called, walking forward slowly. He was alert to any trick the railroad detective might pull.

"Don't shoot me, don't!" whined the detective.

"Get to your damn feet and face me, then," Slocum said. "You can make me shoot you in the back or you can get up and we can do this like men. Your call."

Carlotti struggled to get his feet under him; then he pushed erect. Slocum's slug had grazed him along the right side of his body. Sluggish blood flowed black in the faint moonlight to stain his shirt and coat. The detective turned and squared off.

"I'm right-handed. It's not fair me going for my gun and trying to shoot left-handed."

"That didn't keep you from shooting Cara," Slocum said. "Or are unarmed women the only ones you feel good about shooting?"

"I was aiming at you."

"Did you kill Lily?"

"Who?" Carlotti looked confused at the sudden turn. "I don't know who that is."

Slocum wasn't sure he believed him. But it didn't matter. They were going to settle accounts here and now.

"You've tried to kill me, and you put Cara up to it in Bisbee. I don't care if you think I'm this John Backus you're after or whether you know the truth."

"What truth?"

"I'm not Backus, and you crossed the wrong man."

"Might be I made a mistake. You look a powerful lot like Backus. Leastwise, you fit the description to a fare-thee-well. And there's the similarity of the names."

"Sure," Slocum said, falling into the deadly calmness that preceded a gunfight. "I reckon him and me are the only two men named John in the entire West."

"To me!" shouted Carlotti. "Here he is, men! Backus is here! To me!" As he screamed for help, he was bringing up the small pistol that was standard issue to all of the Arizona Central Railroad detectives. Slocum's response was cool, calculated, and deadly.

He fired when his six-shooter centered on Carlotti's heart. The railroad detective's finger curled on his trigger sending the bullet into the dirt in front of Slocum's boots. Then the man collapsed, as dead as a mackerel.

Slocum walked over, kicked the small-caliber pistol from Carlotti's hand, and then examined the body. He had his battered wallet and gold badge stuffed into a pocket. Slocum realized it had been a mistake flashing those at the Arizona Central Railroad headquarters, but he hadn't had much choice at the time. He plucked wallet and badge from the dead man and thrust them into his inner coat pocket over his heart. There wasn't any purpose to leaving badge for Norbert Peake, as he had done with Sheriff Yarrow and the gun of Boots Wyman in Bisbee, but the badge might come in handy.

From Carlotti's last words, the only one who could call off the manhunt for John Backus—John Slocum—was the owner of the Arizona Central Railroad. Giving him proof of his detective's failure was not likely to convince a rich, powerful man accustomed to getting his own way. Slocum hesitated, wondering if speaking with Peake's wife might not be a better course. Cara had said that Mrs. Peake had hired Backus to kill Leonore Zemansky to get rid of her husband's mistress. Norbert Peake had found out his wife's perfidy and set his murderous bloodhounds onto Backus's trail to exact revenge.

Slocum's reverie was disturbed by the sound of bullets whizzing through the air all around his head. He spun, went into a crouch, and fired without even knowing who attacked him. His first bullet missed, but the second caught a railroad detective in the forearm, causing him to yelp like a stuck pig. This slowed the others with him and gave Slocum the chance to hightail it into the shadows. He doubled back into the garbage pits, then circled Loosey Lucy's brothel and found his horse. He swung into the saddle, only to duck when a new fusillade sought his hide.

Galloping away produced confused cries behind him for him to stop, for others to cut him down, to take him alive so he could stand trial, to tie a noose and string him up. Slocum thought he recognized the Yuma marshal's voice in the middle of the cacophony. That meant not only the railroad detectives were hot on his trail, but Marshal Tennent as well. Getting away from a posse of so many men anxious to ventilate his hide wasn't going to be easy.

Slocum galloped until his horse was about ready to collapse, and he had yet to get very far out of town. He heard a train whistle and saw the tracks not too far off. The train was just leaving Yuma, heading back toward Tucson and El Paso. With luck, Slocum might make it back to Bisbee if he could get as far as the siding at Tucson. He dismounted, got what he needed from the saddlebags, then found a spiny length of cholla cactus.

"Sorry, but I've got to do this." Slocum lifted the saddle blanket and shoved the bristly shaft under the saddle so it would irritate the horse and keep it running until it dropped from exhaustion. Slocum watched it race into the night, neighing as it went. It was a shame to do that to a horse, even one he had technically stolen, but it might put the marshal's posse on the wrong track for hours.

The train vented another whistle blast and began to pick up speed. Slocum ran for all he was worth, grabbed, and let his fingers curl around a cool iron rod. Not enough. The train sped up just enough so he lost his grip and slipped free. He stumbled, then put on a burst of speed equal to that of his now-long-gone aggrieved horse. This time he got a better purchase on the iron handrail and pulled himself up onto the back platform of the caboose. He sat for several minutes, catching his breath and letting the distance increase between him and Yuma.

He considered boldly walking through the caboose and into the train beyond. This time there were four passenger cars and only one freight car, probably carrying the horses for the passengers. But Slocum didn't have two nickels to rub together and had not bought a round-trip fare in Bisbee. He let out a low, heartfelt laugh. Let the railroad detectives find him now! If they did, they'd want him for something more than stealing a free ride on a passenger train.

Scrambling up a ladder, he got to the roof of the caboose and peered into the window in the cupola atop it. Light from inside showed two men playing cards at a small table. Their bunks were up near the top of the caboose, just under the windows. Walking as quietly as he could, Slocum made his way to the freight car in front of the caboose and jumped across the narrow gap between cars. He missed his step and fell heavily. As he began sliding off, he scrambled for purchase. His fingers missed and so did his feet, sending him plunging over the side.

He twisted in midair and grabbed wildly, getting his arm through another of the handrails mounted on the side. He was jerked around and slammed hard into the side of the splintery car, but was still on the train. Shoulder hurting like hellfire, he swung about and got his feet onto the iron rungs so he could reach the roof. From there he opened the hatch and dropped into the freight car. Four horses rode there, but they began putting up a fuss at having a stranger among them.

"Fine, then." Slocum said to them, leaving them to their paltry stalls as he decided to ride like he owned the train rather than hiding in the freight car. Regaining the roof through the hatch, he made his way along to the last of the passenger cars. A quick jump brought him to the narrow loading platform. He peered in the window and smiled. A sleeping car. Six small compartments were outfitted as bedrooms for the richer among the Arizona Central Railroad's patrons. He opened the door and gingerly stepped inside. Whether the rooms were filled wasn't his concern. He wanted to wait for the conductor to finish making the rounds, punching tickets and taking money, then settle down where he wasn't likely to be disturbed for the rest of the trip. Slocum had watched how the conductor had acted before. After that single round of ticket-taking, he would go to the caboose to drink and gamble with the others in the train crew.

Slocum started down the narrow corridor, intending to go to the platform between the sleeping and passenger cars and swing up onto the roof and wait for the conductor to pass below. When the conductor was done, Slocum would find a seat in the passenger car and grab a few hours of much-deserved sleep.

He froze when he saw the door opening in front of him. The conductor's hand was curled around the doorknob as he hesitated before entering. It was too late for Slocum to backtrack and return to the freight car, and he certainly didn't have the money for the trip. With his horse out in the middle of the desert, it would be a long walk to Bisbee— especially with a posse on his heels.

The door opened farther as Slocum began retracing his path down the narrow corridor. He couldn't make it outside in time not to be seen, but had to try. Just as he was sure the conductor was going to spot him, the sleeping room door next to him opened and a hand reached out, grabbed his arm, and pulled him inside.

"Belle!"

The lovely blonde grinned at him. She wore a thin cotton robe with a floral pattern and, from the way it hung open in front, nothing more. The tiny bed was mussed, showing she had been sleeping.

"I wondered who was crashing around outside like a bull in a china shop. I never expected to see you."

Slocum stiffened when he heard the steady steps of the conductor coming down the passageway.

"Don't worry, John," she said. "I'll take care of it." She grinned even more broadly and pressed against him, her robe falling open to reveal what Slocum had suspected. Belle wore nothing under her robe but her birthday suit. In a husky voice she added, "I'll take care of everything." Her hand fleetingly brushed across his groin, then went to the doorknob.

"Ticket, please," called the conductor.

"Here it is," Belle said opening the door the barest fraction. "I do declare. You won't be disturbin' me again, will you? I'm tryin' to get my beauty sleep."

"Ma'am, if it's not too forward, you're already 'bout the purtiest woman alive. You git any purtier, there won't be 'nuff room on this train for all yer admirers."

"You are so sweet," Belle said. "Now you won't disturb me again, will you?"

"No, ma'am, won't do a thing like that, not till we get to Bisbee, if thass what you want."

"Thank you." Belle closed the door and turned, putting her back against it. She shrugged so the robe fell down onto her shoulders, revealing the pale alabaster globes of her breasts—and luscious sights even lower on her body. Slocum saw the slight dome of her belly and the tangled bush peeking out from between her legs. He responded physically in spite of the shock at seeing her on the train.

And the way they had parted company in Bisbee.

When he didn't say anything, she drew away slightly, pressing her entire back against the doorway.

"You're mad at me, aren't you? I'm sorry about what I did, John. That wasn't right, but I did it for your own good."

"How's putting a knockout drug in my drink supposed to be helpful?"

"Why, you needed rest. You had been through so much, and you're not the kind of man who enjoys taking it easy, even when you need to. I see that your sunburn is mostly gone." She ran her hands down his chest, cleverly unbut-

toning his vest and pushing up the shirt to expose bare
skin. Her fingers were cool and arousing as they combed
through the thick mat of chest hair.

"So you did it for my own good?" Slocum wasn't buying this for an instant.

"Just like I hid you from the conductor, John."

"What do you want?" Slocum asked.

"All I want for you is . . . what I want for myself!" Belle
shrugged and let the robe fall to the floor so she stood glo-
riously naked before him. Her arms went around his neck
and pulled his face down to hers for a long, deep kiss that
took away her breath. When she broke off, she was flushed
and gasping. Her face changed subtly as she looked from
his face to points lower. Belle worked to drop his gun belt,
and then expertly opened the buttons on his fly.

Slocum almost gasped with relief when his erection
popped out. It had been trapped in a cloth prison and had
begun to hurt from its cruel imprisonment. He did gasp
when Belle took him in hand, working up and down
slowly. The warmth of her hand spread throughout his
loins, tightening him even more. Slocum bent down and
kissed her. Their lips brushed lightly, then crushed with
growing passion.

Slocum moved even closer and felt her large breasts
crush against his chest. Without breaking off the kiss, he
stripped off his vest, but had to back off a step to remove
his shirt. Belle dropped to her knees and helped get off his
boots and skin down his pants. He looked down at the top
of her blond head.

"While you're there," he suggested, stepping back. As
she turned to look up at him, he thrust with his hips. The
rubbery tip of his organ danced along her half-parted lips.
She smiled wickedly and took the purpled arrowhead tip
into her mouth. He went weak in the knees as she tried to
suck the innards out of him. Lacing his fingers through her
hair, he guided her head back and forth so she took his
fleshy shaft in exactly the rhythm he desired most. He felt
her hot breath gusting across his flesh, her tongue laving

him, her even white teeth lightly scoring the sides of his steely pillar as he moved in and out of her face.

Then he realized she was getting him too excited too fast. Slocum pulled away, reached down, and lifted so the naked woman was on her feet and facing him again.

"More," he said. "I want more."

"I was giving it to you," Belle protested.

"Not like this," he said, reaching down and running his fingers along the sleek flesh of her right buttock. His fingers danced downward, went behind her naked thigh, and then lifted. This allowed Slocum to step in even closer as she opened her most intimate regions to him. Belle immediately understood and looped her leg around his waist, circling his body. As she tightened her muscles, Slocum moved forward, parted her pink hidden lips, and then sank a few inches into her seething hot core.

"Oh!" She tried to throw her head back, but was stopped by the wall. Slocum slid even deeper into her. Belle tensed her leg and held him tightly in place, as if he wanted to move.

In this position, she was up on the toes of one foot while the other was locked behind him. Inch by inch Slocum slid the rest of the way into her center.

"Move, John, more, give it all to me!"

Slocum didn't answer. He simply stood and let the rolling motion of the train rock them to and fro. The vibration and the sideways turns as the train took gentle curves gave them both more stimulation than either expected. Slocum added to it by fondling Belle's fine breasts, kissing her earlobes before gently nipping, then moving along the line of her shoulder until he could not reach any farther. In the moonlight pouring through the window, it looked as if his lips left trails of quicksilver on her silky smooth flesh. But more than this visual thrill, there came the sound of the woman's soft moans, the clatter of steel wheels, and the stabs of increasingly intense sensation shooting into Slocum's loins.

He ran his hands down Belle's sides, cupped her buttocks, and then lifted powerfully. He spun and lost his balance when the train hit a rough patch of rail. But they ended up on the bed, Belle's legs spread wantonly, and Slocum nestled between them. They had never come apart from when their bodies joined. Now Belle's knees rose to either side of his body as he positioned himself for the final act of their lovemaking.

"Fast, John, make it hard and fast. I need it so."

He silenced her with kisses and then lifted enough so that he could ram forward with his hips. The first powerful stroke lifted Belle's tight, taut rump off the bed. She clung fiercely to him, eyes closed and her face bathed in the moonlight filtering through the dirty window of the sleeping compartment.

Never had he seen a woman so desirable. He bent low and dragged his tongue across the hard nubs capping either of her breasts, felt the rubbery snap to them and the frenzied pulsation of her distant heart. He sucked first one and then the other into his mouth and bit gently. Belle let out a cry of sheer animal need, arched her back, and ground her crotch into his.

Slocum almost lost control. He held on until the woman's ecstasy had died, then began the rhythmic motion that built carnal heat along the entire length of his delightfully hidden shaft. Coupled with the swaying sensations of the railcar as it swung about in its trip through the night, Slocum's movement built Belle's passions to the breaking point again. Along with his.

Slocum felt the heat of a volcanic explosion mounting deep inside, and tried to hold off as long as he could to give them both newer and better stimulation by rotating his hips as well as shoving forward with increasingly feverish strength. Soon enough he could not hold back and lost all control.

"Oh, John, oh, so nice," Belle groaned out. Then she bit her lower lip and thrashed about under him as he was tossed about on winds of passion blowing with hurricane fury.

He spilled his seed and then sank down atop the woman. In the small bed there was hardly room enough for the both of them. Neither objected to the closeness.

They lay with arms and legs wrapped around one another, not saying a word. Slocum was exhausted from the day of fighting and loving, but his mind kept turning over all the times he had been with Belle. He couldn't help thinking he was riding a train on a one-way trip.

But what a trip it was. All the way to Bisbee.

18

"I'm hungry," Belle Wilson said, stretching like a cat in the warm sunlight spilling through the sleeping car window. Slocum watched the ebb and flow of her muscles, the sleek flesh, the sheer beauty of the woman he had sampled so avidly all the way from Yuma. There had been little enough to brag on in that town. He had left bodies in his wake and questions unanswered, but with Belle here and Bisbee only a few miles down the line, he had the feeling of getting close to resolution.

"I'll see what I can rustle up."

"You don't have a ticket," she said, sitting up in the bed. She made no attempt to hide her nakedness. If anything, she flaunted it. At another time, Slocum would have been held like a magnet holds iron, but not now, not after the nonstop lovemaking all the way across the Arizona desert.

"So? I'll see if there are any peddlers."

"There always are, but that doesn't mean the conductor'll let you stay on. I'll go."

"Like that?"

Belle looked down at her bare chest, cupped her own breasts, and gave them a little bounce.

"What's wrong with me like this?"

"Nothing—and nothing I'd want to share with the rest of the passengers. Like the conductor said, you ride this line often enough, there won't be an empty seat on the train."

Belle laughed, swung her legs off the bed, and began dressing, humming a tune to herself. As cramped as the compartment was, Slocum managed to get into his clothes before she did. He settled his gun belt and waited for her. He knew what he had to do and needed Belle somewhere else to do it.

"There," she said, patting down a few wrinkles in her dress. "Almost presentable."

"Always presentable," he said.

"I—" Belle bit off her words, then said, "You might be right, John. You should go. I wouldn't feel right leaving you here in the compartment. If the conductor found you, he'd think you were a thief. There's no telling what he might do then. But if he only caught you without a ticket, well, I could pay the fare."

"I suppose so," he said. "Lend me a dollar or two and I'll see about getting some food."

"We could wait. We're not far from Bisbee. I know a good restaurant there."

"I'll see what I can find. My belly's grinding hard against my backbone and my hands are shaking."

"That's not all that was shaking, all the way from Yuma," Belle said, her eyes dancing.

Slocum slipped from the compartment and immediately went toward the freight car. He stepped out on the back platform, took a deep breath, and jumped, hitting the ground hard and rolling to a halt before he plowed into a clump of prickly pears. He got up, dusted himself off, and then started hiking along behind the train. None of the crew had seen him leave the train, and it couldn't be more than an hour into Bisbee on foot. He had business that didn't include Belle Wilson.

Slocum ached all over by the time he reached the outskirts of Bisbee, but he hardly noticed. The festive atmosphere of the town was still obvious by the banners and bunting hanging over the main street. The miners had come in for Norbert Peake's visit and had stayed, getting progressively drunker. When Slocum saw Sheriff Yarrow, he dropped to a chair in front of a saloon and pulled down his hat to cover his eyes, tipped the chair back, and pretended to be asleep. The lawman had three drunk, staggering miners in tow, leading them toward the town jail. Yarrow never gave Slocum a second look. When the lawman was out of sight, Slocum got to his feet and wished he could sit a spell longer.

But he couldn't. He had to clear up a powerful lot of questions, and he knew the man who had the answers. Norbert Peake was in his fancy parlor car on a siding at the Bisbee depot.

Slocum reached the station, his steps slower by the minute. Guards patrolled everywhere, protecting not only Peake's special car but also the one attached to it. From what he overheard as the guards walked in the hot sun, that was Mrs. Peake's personal car. Mrs. Peake rated as high as her husband, from the look of it—but with a private car separate from Norbert Peake. Slocum found that suggestive and decided to look into it. He fell into line behind two guards, then hurried to join them when they noticed him.

"Which of you's Wild Bill?" Slocum asked. The two exchanged glances, then shook their heads.

"Who's that supposed to be?" asked the one Slocum pegged to be the leader.

"Don't rightly know. I was supposed to relieve him. The boss wanted to see him and I was supposed to walk his guard route till further notice."

"Were you in the Army?"

"Was," Slocum allowed, without mentioning he had been a captain in the Confederate Army. These three had the look of Yankees about them.

"Don't know this Wild Bill fellow," the leader said. "You got any identification? Don't reckon I've seen you before."

"Just got in," Slocum said. His mind raced, then he took a chance. It had not worked before, but might now. He touched his coat pocket, found Carlotti's wallet, and pulled it out, flipping it open to show the small gold railroad detective's badge.

"I dunno," said the leader, glancing at it and nodding. "We was supposed to be here alone."

"You want to go check with somebody higher up?" Slocum knew the man would do this very thing. By him suggesting it, everything sounded on the up and up.

The man licked his lips and smiled just a little too much.

"That's a real good idea. I'll track the son of a bitch down. Last I saw him he was in the saloon down the street."

"You just want to get outta this sun," grumbled his partner. "It's killin' me it's so hot."

"You and him stay," the leader said. "Won't take me ten minutes. Maybe fifteen, then we'll have somebody to spell us. Even if none of us is named Wild Bill." The tall, gangly man started off, singing a bawdy tune.

"We might as well settle into a routine," the remaining guard said, wiping his lips on a dusty sleeve. "You just gave him reason to drink every saloon 'tween here and Tucson dry."

"I'm just doing my duty," Slocum said, secretly gloating that it had been so easy to remove one of the men. Sending the other on a fool's errand wouldn't be that much harder, but he had to do it quick if he wanted to poke around.

"Not fair," grumbled the guard. "He shouldn't leave us in the sun like this."

"I could sure use a nip, too," Slocum said. "How about you? This is thirsty work, and you were dead on about it being damned hot in the sun."

"I could use a shot or two of whiskey," the guard allowed.

"Go get a bottle. Or at least something. I'll keep a sharp eye out. You can get back before your partner's talked to the boss." Slocum watched carefully and saw he had hit the nail on the head.

"The nearest saloon's not that far," the guard said thoughtfully, talking himself into leaving Slocum alone.

Then he grinned, showing a broken front tooth. "Who's gonna try anything in this heat? You keep an eye peeled, and I'll be back quicker 'n two shakes of a lamb's tail."

Slocum waited until the man started for the main street where the saloons lined up like soldiers at a parade, then hurried to the second parlor car—Mrs. Peake's. He started to knock, then deciding on a bolder course of action, pushed open the door and went inside, closing the door quickly behind him.

"John!" the woman cried, surprising Slocum. He swung around and faced her. For a moment, she simply stared. Then she fumbled on the small writing desk, put on eyeglasses, and peered more closely at him. "You're not my John! Who are you?"

"My name's Slocum, ma'am, and I have spent the past week or two being confused for John Backus." He saw the flow of emotion across her face and began figuring out what was happening. "Was he a special . . . friend?"

"What an interesting way of putting it," she said briskly, dropping her glasses back to the desk. Up close, Slocum decided that Mrs. Peake was a handsome woman, but not a pretty one. She had the presence, the airs, of a woman who would be perfectly at home at some fancy-dress ball on Nob Hill in San Francisco or some high-society event in Washington, D.C. Slocum saw why Norbert Peake had married her. She would be elegant and eloquent and witty at precisely the right times when he needed her. But she wasn't a beauty.

"Where is Backus?" Slocum asked.

The woman did not answer directly. She picked up a small fan, opened it, and carefully fanned herself before speaking.

"Do you work for Norbert?"

"Fact is, he's set his detectives to kill me. I suspect it's because I look like Backus."

"That's quite possible," the woman said, continuing to fan herself slowly. She looked at him over the rim of the fan in an almost coquettish fashion. "You aren't related to him, are you? To John? No? You look like a brother."

"The handsome brother, I hope," Slocum said, eliciting a laugh from the woman.

"You have a much keener wit than he does. One can only wonder if your other traits are not also more . . . developed."

Slocum felt the pressure of time on him. He looked out the window to see if either of the guards had returned. If the tall, gangly one returned and didn't see his partner, it would be all over. The alarm would be raised, and Slocum might have to shoot his way out. He certainly didn't cotton much to the idea of using the railroad magnate's wife as a shield to get free, as much because he didn't hide behind any woman's skirts as because he might lose all chance of finding out what was going on.

And maybe even who killed Lily Montrechet.

"There's a detective named Carlotti who tried to ventilate me," said Slocum. "He's dead."

"He is? Good," she said with some venom. "You are a better gunman than Mr. Backus, I see."

"Backus killed a woman named Leonore Zemansky. At your order."

"Yes, he did. That slut was seeing my husband, and I don't mean socially."

"Was Lily Montrechet also your husband's mistress? In that small house on the other side of the depot?" He saw the set to her jaw and knew it was true. The clothing in the drawer, carrying Lily's scent, *had* been hers. Did this mean Belle was also one of Norbert Peake's seemingly endless string of mistresses? She had been at the house without actually living there.

"Did Backus kill her, too? Did you order him to kill Lily?" If he had, Slocum found himself on the same side of the fence as Norbert Peake's killers. They had gone after John Backus because he had killed Leonore. If Backus had also killed Lily, he couldn't run far enough for him to hide from Slocum's justice.

Six-gun justice.

"John vanished soon after he killed that Zemansky woman. I haven't seen him since. He might not have been all that bright, but he looked after his own self-interest. He knew Carlotti was after him."

Slocum believed her. He also believed there was something else she wasn't telling him.

"Did your husband hire Boots Wyman and his gang?"

"I don't know whom you mean. Oh, wait, Norbert mentioned them. Bounty hunters, I think. No, they came because of the outrageous reward Norbert offered to kill John when Carlotti could not find him. That may be why he left so quickly."

"When?"

"Why, right after he killed that whore. I told you that."

"You think he might have killed Lily Montrechet, too?" Slocum tried to place everything in order, but it didn't come out quite right. If Mrs. Peake was telling the truth, Backus had hightailed it long before Lily had been murdered.

"Why, no, not him. You are going over the same ground, sir." She quailed when she saw his expression. Slocum considered her as guilty of Leonore's death as the man she had sent to murder the woman. And she had every reason to be responsible for hiring other killers to remove Lily from her husband's bed—permanently.

Again Slocum had the feeling she was not telling something important.

"Will you tell your husband that I'm not this John Backus? I'm tired of looking over my shoulder, waiting for his hired guns to shoot me."

"What are you suggesting? That we go to his little love hovel and have me confess I took John Backus as a lover and you are not him?" Mrs. Peake laughed harshly. "Norbert would never believe me. He'd say I only tried to save your life because I was having an affair with you, as if he hasn't had a string of hussies in his bed."

"Why was Leonore Zemansky important to kill if he's

acted that way since you were married?" Slocum could not figure out the minds of the rich.

"Why, she threatened to shame me publicly. Blackmail. She was going to tell everyone Norbert was divorcing me to marry her. She was quite insane, but it got me to thinking how to prevent this in the future. If she were no longer able to make such wild claims, Norbert would be more circumspect in his affairs."

"So you had Leonore Zemansky killed?"

"What was your name again? Mr. Slocum? Mr. Slocum, please believe me, I had no interest in involving you in what is essentially a private matter."

"Private? You've got armies of gunmen killing each other!" He had reached the end of his patience. "Come on. We'll go talk to your husband. He'll either believe me or I'll leave his carcass in the desert for the buzzards."

"You will *not*!" she said indignantly. "I love my husband, and you will not harm a hair on his head."

"Come on," Slocum said. He wanted this over and done, and he wanted to find out who had ended Lily's life. If it hadn't been Mrs. Peake's lover, Backus, then he still had a long road ahead of him finding the real killer.

"Very well, but this will end badly for us all," she said. She folded her fan and placed it carefully on the edge of her writing desk, then picked up her broad-brimmed hat and adjusted it painstakingly until Slocum wanted to simply shoot her and be done with it. The woman finally satisfied herself that the hat was properly placed, then allowed Slocum to open the door leading out into the blast furnace hot Arizona heat.

"Mrs. Peake, where you goin'?"

Slocum cursed under his breath. The second guard had returned, trying to hide the whiskey bottle from his boss's wife.

"You ain't supposed to go out unescorted."

"I'm escorting her," Slocum said before the woman could respond. In a lower voice, Slocum added, "Stay here.

You'll have plenty of time to wet your whistle. Just save some for me."

"This is all right with the boss?"

"It is," Mrs. Peake said irritably. This satisfied the guard. With the bottle held behind him, he wasn't inclined to ask any more questions. They walked off in the intense heat that sapped Slocum's strength if not his resolve.

"There it is," Slocum said, steering the woman toward the small house where Cara had been taken after getting shot and where he had met Belle Wilson for the first time. He wondered what Belle's connection was to the railroad tycoon. He asked.

"Is Belle Wilson one of his mistresses, too?"

Slocum thought he had poked the woman with a pin. She jumped, tried to cover her surprise, then emphatically shook her head.

"The only two I've known were that Yuma slut and the brassy chanteuse."

Slocum wanted to pursue this, but they had reached the front of the house. He started to knock, then decided the hell with it and kicked open the door. It slammed hard against the inside wall, almost coming off its hinges. He pushed Mrs. Peake ahead of him and then stepped to one side. Norbert Peake sat at the small table, a simple meal spread in front of him. From the direction of the bedroom came sounds of someone stirring, then hurriedly getting dressed.

"What the hell is the meaning of this?" demanded the railroad magnate.

"Stay in your chair," Slocum said. "If you go for that hideout gun of yours, I'll shoot you where you sit."

"What? This is an outrage! Norbert, I had no idea—"

"Shut up," Peake snapped.

"I need some answers, and I don't much care how I get them," Slocum said, his six-shooter in his hand but not pointing at either the man or the woman. More sounds from the bedroom told of a frightened woman there. Norbert Peake had a new mistress for his little Bisbee love nest. Slocum guessed he had houses like this in every city along the Arizona Central Railroad line.

"This is no way to proceed, sir," Peake said, glaring at him. "I don't know why my men haven't caught you already, but I assure you they will."

"You think I'm John Backus, don't you?" Slocum snorted in disdain. "I killed Carlotti in a fair fight, and walked away unscathed when Boots Wyman was gunned down." Slocum's mind turned to that night and the incredible shot someone had made, robbing Wyman of his life with the same one-shot skill that had taken Lily Montrechet.

"You match the description."

"Backus left the territory after he killed Leonore Zemansky," Slocum said. "He's not likely to ever show his face here again. I just happen to look like him. And I was with Lily when those owlhoots shot up the theater in Tombstone and we hightailed it. She wanted to come here, probably to ask for your protection." Slocum saw Peake preparing to lie. He added an arrow to the man's already wounded veracity. "She thought you'd help her, Big Willie."

Norbert Peake suddenly looked like a fish out of water. His mouth opened and closed a couple times; then he swallowed hard. Slocum had made his point. He had known Lily well enough for her to tell him everything.

"What shoot-out?" Norbert Peake said trying to recover his composure.

"The one in Tombstone, you fool," Mrs. Peake said. "I wanted to be certain you got the message. What's this about 'Big Willie'? That is not a description of *you*!"

Norbert Peake glared at his wife. She shrugged and tried to look innocent; then her anger flared.

"John killed that whore and then disappeared, so I got someone else to finish the chore of killing all your sluts, Norbert. I see that there's not enough ammunition west of the Mississippi for that now, but that won't prevent who I hired from trying. You've cheated on me for the last time, Norbert." Mrs. Peake stared daggers at the bedroom when the woman there gasped. The window creaked open and the rustle of skirts told of Peake's new mistress choosing to abandon her lover rather than have his wife's hired killer add her to the death roster.

"You were having an affair with Backus," Peake said. "What did you think I'd do about that? Thank him for screwing my wife behind my back?"

"Shut up," Slocum snapped. "You had nothing to do with Lily's death?" He directed the question at Norbert Peake.

"Of course not. She was a fine woman, one of the best. I assume you understand fully what I mean."

"You filthy beast!" shrieked his wife, launching herself at him. He batted away her clawing hands, grabbed her wrists, and held her, then continued to speak to Slocum as if there hadn't been a distraction.

"Lily was talented and understanding of the way our . . . relationship had to be. Of course I didn't have her killed."

"Then *she* did," Slocum said, staring at Peake's wife. "That's what she meant when she said she wanted to be sure you got the message."

"What if she did? It was only because she loves me."

"Who killed her? Who did you hire to murder Lily?" Slocum asked the wife, fighting to keep his anger in check. For two bits he would plug both of them. He lifted his six-gun, then froze. Something hard and round poked into his spine. He sucked in a deep breath and caught a hint of familiar perfume, one he associated with men being gunned down.

"I'll take care of this," came a familiar voice. "You two have so much to talk over."

"Who's that?" demanded Peake. "I can't see who's there."

"Oh, dear, don't worry about that," said Mrs. Peake. "She's right. We should let bygones be bygones. Maybe we can even see how comfy that bed back there is, since that hussy back there is gone."

"No," came Belle's command to Slocum as he started to

whirl about. "Don't try it." She reached around and plucked the six-gun from his hand. "Outside, John. Now."

He let her push him into the hot Arizona sun, then close the door behind her the best she could. He glanced over his shoulder. Belle held the six-shooter on him as if she knew how to use it.

"Lady Death," he said.

"Oh, my, I was afraid Wyman would say something silly like that. He was such a foolish man. But it has a certain ring to it, don't you think? Lady Death. It wins me many jobs without having to go through tedious interviews."

"Did Cara work for you?"

"Of course not. I do my own . . . chores. She was a silly little bitch who thought she was doing Carlotti a favor. She mistook you for John Backus since there is such a remarkable resemblance. Quite uncanny, actually. At least in your features. You two are so different in the ways that matter."

"So Carlotti, Cara, Wyman, and his gang were all trying to gun down Backus for Norbert Peake. Backus killed Leonore because Mrs. Peake asked him to."

"And they were lovers, yes. He was quite smitten with her. I think she was only using him for her own ends."

Belle sounded smug, but Slocum had reached an inescapable conclusion.

"You killed Lily for Mrs. Peake. She hired you and you gunned her down."

"Yes," Belle Wilson said in a voice so soft and low it was almost swallowed by the wind whipping over the desert. "It didn't quite work out the way I had originally planned. Those two gunmen I hired in Tombstone were supposed to kill her, making it look like a drunken hurrah gone wrong. That would have kept any suspicion of premeditation from surfacing, as if the law would care. But Norbert Peake has a way of making people do what he wants. You prevented the gunmen from killing Lily, and I had foolishly not prepared to finish the job they started. Not until later, when I tracked you two down and found you by the watering hole."

"You're a dead woman, Belle." Slocum's fury threatened to explode and make him do something foolish. He knew how deadly accurate a marksman she was, and it hardly mattered. He wanted to strangle her with his bare hands for killing Lily.

"Remember, John, I also saved your life twice. Who do you think cut you free? And then I killed Wyman before he could shoot you."

"I don't remember it happening that way," he said. She had murdered Lily and she had murdered Wyman. How many others?

"Let's walk," she said. "I have a little thinking to do."

"On how to kill me?"

"I am afraid so," she said. "Mrs. Peake would be wroth with me if I actually killed John Backus, but she knows you are someone else entirely. And Mr. Peake is quite a generous man. With what Mrs. Peake paid me to kill Lily and what Norbert will pay to kill you, why, it would be enough to live in high society for quite some time."

Slocum walked, mind racing.

"Or I could simply let you go. We did have quite a time together."

"You thought I was Backus," he said.

Belle Wilson laughed.

"You're so clever, John. Yes, I admit it. I thought you were Mrs. Peake's lover at first. I actually congratulated her on such a fine paramour, too, never thinking you were someone else."

"You were saving me for her."

"Now that everyone knows you're not Backus, that's no longer necessary."

They walked across the tracks and went deeper into the desert south of town. Slocum slowed the pace, knowing Belle would have no hesitation about killing him when they were out of sight of the station agent and anyone else around the depot.

"Lady Death," he said.

"So melodramatic, but I am glad you appreciate my position. I do so wish I could keep you, but that's like keeping a pet rattlesnake in bed with me. So pretty, but sooner or later you make a mistake and he bites you fatally."

Slocum heard Belle's six-gun cock.

"Hey, you two want to share a bit of my whiskey?" came the loud call.

Slocum spun and tried to grab her gun, but her reactions were too quick. She pulled the trigger of her six-gun. He felt a sudden shock in his chest, rocking him back. He stumbled and dropped to his knees.

"What's goin' on?" the guard cried. He went for his six-shooter as Belle turned on him.

Lady Death. Drunken guard. Two more shots. Belle was deadly accurate, and the guard's luck had run out.

Slocum moaned and pulled his coat away from his body. Belle's bullet had drilled through Carlotti's badge and pressed metal into his flesh. Tiny beads of blood oozed around the pieces as he pulled it free and cast it away. He pulled the derringer he had taken from Cara, aimed, and fired. Twice. Belle never let out a sound as she died.

For a long minute Slocum lay on the ground, garnering his strength. Only then did he get to his feet and stumble to where Belle lay. Even in death she was lovely.

Slocum picked up his six-shooter and shoved it into his holster. Then he threw down the derringer and, on shaky legs, walked back to the train station where other railroad detectives were congregating, trying to figure out what the shooting was all about.

"What's goin' on?" demanded the gangly guard.

"There, dead," Slocum said, pointing in the direction of the other guard and Belle's bodies. The detectives ran off, leaving Slocum behind. He pressed his hand into the wound on his chest, winced, then looked around and found a pair of horses tethered nearby. He swung into the saddle of one and scooped up the reins of the other. With a pair of horses and a decent head start, he could be across the border into Mexico before anyone noticed he was gone.

Horse stealing was a serious crime, but Slocum reckoned Norbert Peake and his wife owed him for not killing the pair of them when he could have. He rode hard and fast, leaving behind Bisbee, crossing the border, getting into the central mountains of Mexico before stopping. Even then he didn't feel that he was far enough away or ever would be.

Watch for

SLOCUM AND THE SULFUR VALLEY WIDOWS

320TH novel in the exciting SLOCUM series
from Jove

Coming in October!